He leaned forward and the movement caught her off guard. "If all goes well on this date, I'm hoping it ends in an intimate nightcap." His eyes dropped to her lips again, but this time, he didn't hide the heat behind his gaze.

Did he just suggest what I think he suggested?

She didn't know whether to curse him out or kiss him senseless. The way he quirked his mouth to the side in a smile made her want to see what he had behind his smize. On the other hand, the fact that she immediately had naughty thoughts about a mouth that belonged to a guy who didn't care enough about the date to be on time—and then had the nerve to look sexy as hell—made her want to give him a tongue-lashing and *not* the toe-curling kind. So she opted for the latter.

"You have some nerve," she said as she leaned closer to him. "First, you show up almost an hour late. Then we barely hold a conversation and when we do speak, it's about things we already know about one another. Next, you suggest that we have an intimate nightcap when you've barely put in any work to get me into your bed."

Dear Reader,

I'd like to introduce you to the Dupree sisters, owners of Bare Sophistication lingerie boutique and the cousins of my Elite Events series heroes—Micah Madden (*Red Velvet Kisses*) and Malik Madden (*Beautiful Surrender*). *Enticing Winter* also features Taheim Reed who was introduced in my debut Harlequin Kimani Romance novel, *A Tempting Proposal*.

I knew the minute Winter and her sisters opened their Chicago boutique, the gorgeous free spirit would be the perfect match for Taheim. Both characters may appear to be total opposites, but as you will learn, they have more in common than they think.

Autumn's story is next and I can't wait for you to see what's in store for her! She lives her life in facts, not fiction. However, this realist may soon meet her match.

Much love,

Sherelle

authorsherellegreen@gmail.com
@sherellegreen

Enticing
Winter

Sherelle Green

HARLEQUIN® KIMANI™ ROMANCE

Recycling programs
for this product may
not exist in your area.

ISBN-13: 978-0-373-86422-5

Enticing Winter

Printed in U.S.A.

Sherelle Green is a Chicago native with a dynamic imagination and a passion for reading and writing. Her love for romance developed in high school after stumbling across a hot and steamy Harlequin novel. She instantly became an avid romance reader and decided to pursue an education in English and journalism. A true romantic, she believes in predestined romances, love at first sight and fairy-tale endings.

Books by Sherelle Green

Harlequin Kimani Romance

A Tempting Proposal
If Only for Tonight
Red Velvet Kisses
Beautiful Surrender
Enticing Winter

Visit the Author Profile page at Harlequin.com for more titles.

Dedication

To my aunts and uncles who have constantly supported me in all my endeavors. I honestly cannot thank each of you enough for all your encouragement and guidance. There is nothing in the world greater than knowing I can depend on my family for any and everything.

I love you all…from the bottom of my heart!

Acknowledgments

To my cousin Daniel "Danny" for inspiring the character of Taheim Reed. You're so ambitious and I love your determination. Not only are you always making everyone around you laugh, but I love the fact that you are so family oriented. It's so important to have people in your life that you can count on and you are definitely one of those people for me. Your charismatic spirit and fun-loving personality are what often draw people to you. But you're also private and quiet, always surprising those who may not know you with the way you view a situation or circumstance. It's in those moments that others get to see another side of you, the man that keeps others guessing and loves with his whole heart.

Prologue

Winter looked at her watch for the tenth time in the past forty minutes. "Unbelievable," she huffed as she took out her phone to call her sister Autumn. She answered on the second ring.

"Either your date went terrible or he stood you up."

"Considering he is already forty minutes late, I'm assuming he plans to stand me up."

"Maybe something came up?"

Winter looked at her phone to make sure she had dialed the right number. "Since when are you an optimist? I expected you to tell me to forget about this blind date and go home."

"I'm still half realist, half pessimist. But in this case, since you both share a few mutual friends, I think it's best if you at least wait until he gets there."

"What if he doesn't show?"

"Wait ten more minutes. If he doesn't show, leave."

As she hung up the phone, she still wasn't sure she wanted to wait ten more minutes. Just as she'd made the decision to ignore what Autumn said and leave, she felt as if she was being watched. She turned her head toward the entrance of the restaurant and got lost in the chocolate eyes of a man she hated to admit was worth the wait. Since moving to Chicago two years ago, she'd heard more than a few women comment on Taheim Reed's good looks. Seeing him in person, she now knew firsthand.

He began walking toward the table with a confident stride, gaining the attention of more than a few women.

"Nice to officially meet you, Winter," he said when he reached the table. She glanced down at his outstretched hand, debating whether or not she should accept it.

"You're almost an hour late."

His lips curled into a smile. "I had some business to attend to."

She waited for him to offer more of an explanation. "So, no apology, then?"

He turned his head to the side and motioned for her to take a seat. She thought about ignoring his request but quickly decided she'd rather sit down than give the people sitting next to them something to talk about.

"I apologize. There is no excuse for keeping a woman as beautiful as you waiting."

Hmm, smooth talker. Looks-wise, he was definitely Winter's type. She wasn't really picky. But personality-wise, he was someone she would never go for. She typically fell for musicians or the starving-artist type. Not the conceited playboy. "I accept your apology."

"Great," he said as he took her hand, which was placed on the table. "Now we can get to know each other more."

She wasn't sure what it was about his move that irritated her, but she pulled her hand out of his and picked up the menu, which she'd already memorized in the time she'd waited for him to arrive.

"Are you both ready to order?" the waiter asked when he approached their table. She voiced her order, as did Taheim without even opening his menu.

"You must come here a lot."

He shrugged. "I've been here a few times."

Winter nodded her head as she played with the rim of her glass of water. The awkward silence was unavoidable.

"So what do you do?" he asked as he sat back in his chair.

"I'm one of the owners of Bare Sophistication lingerie boutique in the River North area downtown. What about you?"

"I'm a partner at R&W Advertising and a clothing designer. You may have heard of me," he said, then took a sip of his water. Winter forced her eyes not to drop to his lips. "I just launched my clothing line, Collegiate Life Apparel, early last year."

Of course she'd heard of him. And she was sure that because of the friends they shared, he'd heard of her, too. "Congratulations on your success."

"You, as well," he replied, confirming that he had heard of her boutique even if he hadn't said anything.

His eyes dropped to her lips before making their way back to her face.

"What are your plans after this date?"

I'd barely classify this as a date. And the question was pretty random, even for Winter, who often loved random questions. "Probably working on some new designs. What about you?"

He leaned forward and the movement caught her off guard. "If all goes well, I'm hoping for an intimate nightcap." His eyes dropped to her lips again, but this time, he didn't hide the heat behind his gaze. *Did he just suggest what I think he suggested?*

She didn't know whether to curse him out or kiss him senseless. The way he quirked his mouth to the side made her want to see what he had behind his smize. On the other hand, the fact that she immediately had naughty thoughts about the mouth of a guy who didn't care enough about the date to be on time made her want to give him a tongue-lashing, and *not* the toe-curling kind. So she opted for the latter.

"You have some nerve," she said as she leaned closer to him. "First you show up almost an hour late. Then we barely hold a conversation and when we do speak, it's about things we already know about one another. Next you suggest that we have an intimate nightcap?"

"I apologized for being late," he said, clearly amused by their banter. "And I did plan on asking you more questions. But let's just cut to the chase." He brushed his fingers over her arm and it took all of her energy not to give him the satisfaction of her pulling away again. "We both know how this night is going to end. You're as attracted to me as I am to you."

"Oh, I see," Winter said. "This is how it usually

works for you." She waved her hand back and forth between them. "You take a woman out, spit a few seductive words, and before you know it, you're dragging her back to your place."

He squinted his eyes together as if he was contemplating what she was saying. "Pretty much. I wouldn't proposition you if I couldn't tell you were already interested." He leaned back in his chair. "Until you admit it, too, you're just wasting both of our time."

Who the heck is this guy? "Ha!" she said, finally moving her arm from his touch. "I bet that underneath that arrogant facade is a little boy who was hurt so badly by a woman that he developed this playboy alter ego. When deep down, he's just damaged goods."

She watched the spark behind his gaze leave, and although she wished she didn't, she missed that glimmer of light. She almost wanted to take back her words, but he quickly covered up the fact that she'd gotten to him.

"I heard about you when you got to Chicago," he said with his smirk back in place. "A woman who calls herself a free spirit and doesn't take dating seriously. Maybe you're trying to hide behind the fact that you're scared of a man getting too close to you because when he gets to know the real you, he won't like what he sees."

Taheim inwardly winced at the hurt look on Winter's face. He had no idea what had provoked him to say those words to a woman he barely knew.

Yes, you do, the voice inside his head stated. *She got a little too close to the truth, so instead of being a gentleman and letting it slide, you shot back.*

"I think it's best if we end this so-called date." Their food hadn't even arrived yet, but he knew she was right.

"I agree," he said. "I know the owner, so I'll just cover dinner, even though we didn't eat."

"I can pay for my own dinner," she said, already digging in her purse.

"It's fine, really."

She looked up from her purse. "No, it's fine... really!"

"So now you're just repeating what I say?"

"Not at all. Unlike those other moochers you probably date, I can cover my own dinner."

"I've only dated top-quality women," he said, suddenly defensive.

The side-eye she gave him proved she wasn't buying it. "Fifty bucks says you're lying."

In truth, he didn't always date quality women, but he wouldn't tell her that. Hell, he couldn't remember the last woman he'd dated who actually intrigued his mind. He'd be the first to admit, but not to her, that he thought more with the lower part of his body in regards to the opposite sex.

"I don't know why the ladies of Elite Events thought we would be a good fit."

"Me neither," he agreed. "As soon as I sat down, you'd decided that this date was going to be terrible. My guess is you hate blind dates and I was doomed from the start."

"Me? What about you?" She stopped searching her purse. "You assumed that I would be one of those women you've dated that hangs on to every word you say. Before you even sat at this table, you knew how you were going to approach me. So I think it's safe to say we both agree this date was a mistake."

He studied her facial features, assuming her tenseness mirrored how his own face appeared.

"Hey, Taheim." He turned to the voice he heard behind him.

"Hey, Amanda, how are you?"

"Fine now that I saw you," she said as she leaned slightly toward him, evidently trying to bring his gaze from her face to her chest. "I was hoping you could take me out after you finish up with whatever this is." She flicked her hand toward Winter in disregard.

Taheim chanced a glance at Winter and was unable to miss the knowing look in her eyes. "Just like I said," she replied as she finally pulled out some cash, which she placed on the table for her half of dinner. "The moochers trailing behind you are in full effect tonight, huh?"

"What did you just call me?" Amanda said, pointing a long acrylic nail in Winter's direction.

Winter stood to put on her coat, completely ignoring Amanda.

"I asked you a question."

"Which I ignored," Winter said as she turned to face Amanda. "Listen, I don't care what you and Taheim do after I leave. Regardless of the fact that I can't stand to be at this dinner a minute longer, I could have called you much worse considering that you are the one who came to the table and rudely ignored the fact that I was sitting here."

Amanda flicked her long weave over her shoulder and placed her arm over Taheim's shoulder. "That's because you're irrelevant."

Winter lifted an eyebrow and took two steps toward Amanda. To Taheim's surprise, Amanda actually took a couple steps back. Winter then looked at Taheim and brought her lips closer to his ear.

"Quality women, huh," she whispered. "You owe me fifty bucks."

With that she grabbed her purse and walked out of the restaurant.

"Did she just say I wasn't a quality chick?" Amanda asked as she poked him in the side. "She must have me confused with someone else, because I'm as classy as they come."

She walked over and sat in the seat that Winter had just vacated, in a dress so tight he swore he could see the imprint of her panties. "And since she was so disrespectful, I'll take this money as a consolation for having to listen to her talk crap about me."

As he watched Amanda stuff the cash Winter had placed on the table in her bra, he averted his eyes and winced. Not only had his blind date crashed and burned, but Amanda—a woman whose company often kept him amused—was making him want to run to the nearest exit.

Chapter 1

Three months later

"Angelique, you seriously cannot be doing this to me right now!"

Winter Dupree clutched her smartphone, trying to refrain from throwing it against the wall. "There are thirty women waiting to see you strut your stuff across the hardwood floor in less than an hour."

"I know, Winter, and I'm so sorry," Angelique replied.

"Whoosah." Winter took a deep breath as she stepped deeper into the dimly lit walk-in closet. "Now's the time when you tell me this is just a joke and men dressed in funny costumes are going to throw confetti and yell 'Surprise!'"

She briefly noticed that all the coats and jackets in the closet coordinated with a pair of shoes that were placed right beneath them. *Seriously? Who the heck does that?*

It was bad enough she was hiding in a closet when she was supposed to be hosting a bachelorette party, but now she was also snooping in the closet of a man she'd rather forget existed.

"Our flight takes off in less than ten minutes, so this is definitely not a joke."

"I think your boyfriend surprising you with a trip to Paris is amazing, since his timing is perfect," she said sarcastically. "How about I just tell the client that my top model was swept away on a romantic getaway, so we will show our backless embellished lace baby-doll paired with a pearl lace thong on a dull manne-quin instead."

"Oh, Winter, that would be awesome. I was wor-ried—"

"I was not being serious," Winter said, cutting off the rest of Angelique's sentence. "I'd rather have a root canal than tell a client we can't deliver on what we promised. I'll have to figure something else out."

"Why don't you have another model wear that piece?"

Winter quirked one eyebrow and blinked several times. "I'll pretend like you didn't just say that my cus-tomized piece that was made to fit your measurements exactly could be worn by another model. Those chic black pieces are the signature look for our European-inspired lingerie collection and you are the only model who can pull off the look."

"I'll make it up to you when I get back to Chicago," Angelique said, rushing Winter off the phone. "It's the last boarding call. Talk to you soon!"

Winter dropped her head to the floor as she listened to the silence on the other end of the call. "Ugh! Must be nice to get whisked away on a trip to Paris." She knew she sounded bitter, but at the moment, she didn't care. Angelique was one of her best models. Also the first model who had signed up when word spread through the Chicago fashion industry that Bare Sophistication had decided to throw masquerade lingerie events to promote signature pieces from their store. Winter had been in business with her sisters for over two years now and she was really excited about the direction Bare Sophistication was taking.

She and her sisters had immediately developed a great business model. Winter handled all the visual merchandising and design for the lingerie store. Autumn managed the business and sales, while Summer handled all public relations and advertising despite the fact that she was currently residing in Miami. Their newly appointed manager, Danni Allison, assisted in the daily operations and staff management.

Last month Winter had decided that it was time to bring their boutique to another level. She'd come up with the idea of throwing upscale masquerade lingerie events that offered customized pieces that weren't available in-store and therefore only available if purchased at an elaborate masquerade lingerie party. In addition, they also offered sexy European-inspired nightwear and robes to complement the lingerie.

With the help of her friends at Elite Events Incorporated, Winter had been able to gather a list of Chicago's most influential women. She'd then sent the group of women a special invitation so that those interested could schedule an informational one-on-one meeting to learn more about hosting a Bare Sophistication masquerade lingerie event. Within a week, she had ten events lined up.

"Winter, are you in there?"

Winter cracked the door open and pulled Danni inside the closet. "Angelique can't make the lingerie fashion show tonight."

Danni's eyes grew big with panic, mirroring exactly how Winter felt. Tonight was their first event and Winter's first client, Kaya Reed, was extremely excited to have Bare Sophistication host a lingerie party for her best friend's bachelorette party. Despite the fact that Winter had an adamant dislike for Kaya's older brother Taheim Reed, she had eagerly agreed to help Kaya, who happened to be a sweetheart, throw a party her friend would never forget.

Unfortunately, that included a top-notch lingerie fashion show that ended with the signature piece Kaya was convinced her bestie would appreciate as a bachelorette gift. Which was why it was imperative that she have a model actually try on the best piece in the collection.

"There's absolutely no way she can make it here in time?" Danni asked.

"Nope, her boyfriend surprised her with a trip to Paris."

"Aww, how romantic. I wonder if he'll propose on the trip. I bet Angelique is hoping he proposes. If you had seen the two of them in the store the other day when he picked her up for lunch… They were so cute…"

"Danni," Winter said as she waved a hand in front of her to cut her off. Winter hated being rude, but she had little time to put together a backup plan now that

Angelique was a no-show. "Sorry to cut you off, but we need to focus. Can we switch out any of the models to have them try on the special piece?"

Danni quirked her mouth to the side in thought. "I'm sure we can, but we also chose Angelique because she was similar in size and build to the bride-to-be. That way the bride would have a visual of how she would look before Kaya surprised her with the customized set we made for her."

"I understand, but we may have to make do with another model." Even as the words left her mouth, Winter found it hard to believe them. Oftentimes her sisters teased her about being a go-with-the-flow type of woman. But when she wanted things to go a certain way and plans didn't work out, she could never hide her disappointment.

"You know there's another solution to this problem," Danni said.

"I'm all ears."

Danni averted her eyes as if trying to find the right words. "There's only one woman who is similar to Angelique." Hopeful eyes met Winter's.

"I know you're not suggesting what I think you're suggesting."

"Oh, come on, Winter." Danni tugged on her arm. "You'd look amazing in the piece and you definitely have the shape for it."

"You have got to be kidding me." Winter knew that there would come a time when one of her models would flake on her. But there was absolutely no way she was modeling the lingerie herself.

"I have an image to uphold and modeling in little

to nothing isn't exactly the visual I want to leave for the women in that room."

"Angelique was going to wear a masquerade mask anyway that covered half her face. Even if some of the ladies know it's you, they won't say anything. Plus, half of them are tipsy anyway."

Of course, Winter knew all about the mask since she was the one who'd decided on the look for Angelique. But that wasn't the point.

"Danni, I don't think that's a good idea."

"Do you have a better one?" When Winter remained silent, Danni continued. "Okay, then. Let's get out of this closet and get you ready. The other models are preparing in the bathrooms and spare room on this level, but Kaya said we could use the bedroom upstairs if we need more room."

Reluctantly, Winter let Danni drag her down the hall. She passed a few ladies who spoke about what a great time they were having so far. The minute they walked into the bedroom in the corner of the second level, Winter knew it was Taheim's.

"Is there another room we can use?"

Danni squinted her eyes in confusion. "Don't be silly—this is fine. I have to make sure the ladies are ready since you'll now be in the show instead of running the show." She ushered Winter into the room before turning quickly on her heels. "I'll grab your lingerie outfit and I'll be right back so you can change. Don't worry—you'll be great."

She didn't have a chance to respond before Danni was out the door, leaving her alone in the last place she wanted to be. Large black-and-gray contemporary furniture filled the confines of the spacious bedroom, which was equipped with a water wall and sunken living space.

Of course Mr. Too-Arrogant-for-His-Own-Good has a bedroom to die for. She wouldn't put it past him to have a walk-in closet bigger than her bedroom either. The closet she'd been hiding in earlier was already half the size of her bedroom. As if her feet had a mind of their own, they carried her in the direction of the closet, which began to slide open the minute she stepped in front of it.

"Well, I'll be damned," she said aloud as her hand grazed over the first row of clothing hanging on the lower pole. Just as she'd predicted, his closet was bigger than her entire bedroom. Whenever she thought about Taheim Reed, all that came to mind was complete and utter frustration. The man was a walking nuisance and even though she seemed to be the only woman in Chicago not falling for the playboy, it didn't ease her irritation.

The first time she'd heard about Taheim, she'd been attending an annual networking event thrown by Elite Events Incorporated. While she'd met the Elite Event ladies through her cousins Micah and Malik Madden, that day she'd really bonded with them and had been surprised when they mentioned that they had a friend she would be perfect for.

Winter would rather have had a full-body wax than go on a blind date, but with a little coaxing, she'd agreed to the setup. Fortunately, since she'd been busy getting her company off the ground and Taheim had been promoting his clothing line, they hadn't immediately gotten a chance to go on that date. She'd thought she'd dodged a bullet until her new friends suggested they go out before the first practice for the Elite Events Charity Date Auction, which both she and Taheim were a part of. If she'd known then what she knew now, she would have told them there was no way in hell she was going on a date with Taheim Reed.

Winter left the walk-in closet—which conveniently closed right after she'd exited—and ran her hand across a couple cologne bottles sitting on the top of his dresser. She then moved her hands over his watches. She tilted her head to the side and admired the black watch box, which seemed big enough to hold more than fifty watches. When her eyes landed on the watch he'd been wearing when they'd gone out, her stomach stirred with awareness and something she refused to acknowledge. She thought back to the moment he'd entered the restaurant wearing a business suit, clearly having just come from a meeting. Even though he had been almost an hour late and she'd been ready to leave, she had called her sister Autumn, who'd convinced her to stay.

She'd been caught off guard by his good looks. She'd seen pictures of him, but those photos hadn't done the milk-chocolate Adonis justice.

"Here's the outfit," Danni said, causing Winter to jump, as if Danni could see the direction her naughty mind was going. "If you head down in about fifteen to twenty minutes, that should be fine."

"Okay," Winter mumbled as Danni closed the door behind her. She glanced at the black lace material lying on the bed and the stylish black-and-white masquerade mask that would complete her overall look. She hadn't really modeled since she was in college, but desperate times called for desperate measures. There was no doubt in her mind that the group of women downstairs were ready to purchase one-of-a-kind Bare Sophistication pieces.

"I can't believe I forgot the spare key," Taheim Reed whispered to himself as he tiptoed through the door of his condo and quickly made his way to the flight of stairs leading to the second floor.

When his sister, Kaya, had asked if she could use his condo for her best friend's bachelorette party, Taheim had immediately agreed. Kaya was his heart and there was nothing that he—or his older brother, Ajay—wouldn't do for her, even if that meant having a bunch of tipsy women in his place. So he'd packed an overnight bag and headed to his friend Jaleen's condo so that Kaya could have the freedom to do as she pleased. But forgetting the spare key to his friend's place wasn't part of the plan. Especially since Jaleen was out of town. Now he was sneaking into his own home, attempting to go unseen by his sister or any of the other women in attendance.

When he hit the top of the stairs, he briefly looked over the banister to see if his eyes were playing tricks on him. *What the hell is going on?* he thought as he observed several women strutting around his place in lingerie. He expected to see half-naked women at a bachelor party, but a bachelorette party? It didn't make sense. When he caught a glimpse of Kaya talking to another attractive woman in lace lingerie, he figured it was best if he got the key and exited as quickly as possible.

As he made his way down the hall, he thought about the fact he had never asked Kaya what type of bachelorette party she was throwing. He trusted his sister to be responsible and the last thing he wanted was to hear the details of the type of night she was preparing. Seeing as his condo had turned into a scene right out of a late-night adult reality show, he probably should have asked a few more questions.

He opened the double doors of his bedroom and immediately stopped in his tracks. Standing in the middle of his sunken living room, slowly pulling up a pair of thigh-high stockings, was the sexiest woman he'd ever laid eyes on.

Her back was completely bare with the exception of a pearl thong delicately placed between two plump cheeks he was dying to get his hands on. Her long hair was delicately draped to one side in soft brown curls. The black heels adorning her feet were the type meant to stay on in the bedroom…the kind that appeared in every man's fantasy. Similar to the type of fantasy Taheim was witnessing right now.

He didn't know who this seductress was in his room and damned if he even cared. Obviously, like the other women downstairs, she was participating in whatever was going on for the bachelorette party. But unlike the other women he'd seen, this one made every fiber in his body come to life. What man wouldn't be standing on high alert upon finding an attractive woman half-naked in his bedroom? But that wasn't all that had him salivating over her as if he were a starved man who'd just been told he could have anything on the menu. It was the crazy notion that this woman was in his bedroom for him and him only, his for the taking.

Taheim could definitely have his share of women, but looking at the tempting beauty oblivious to his arrival made him feel as if it had been months since he'd had sex instead of weeks.

She lifted her right leg and slightly bent her back as she tied the black ribbon at the top of her thigh-high stockings. When she lightly adjusted the pearls at the top of the thong, Taheim sucked in a breath, unable to hold back his lust any longer.

He let out a slow whistle as he took a gradual perusal of her body from her thighs and up her back, lingering at the delicate slope of her neck.

At the sound of his voice, she began to slowly turn her head over her left shoulder to the door where he was standing. His heart began beating faster as he waited for her to completely turn around to face where he stood. When she finally did, she gasped in surprise. He was sure her gasp was nothing in comparison to the groan that had escaped his lips.

The black-and-white mask covering half of her face only enticed him more. Who was this woman? And how did he get so lucky as to find her in his bedroom? He was so busy taking in his fill of her that he almost didn't realize that she was removing her mask. He waited in anticipation as inch by inch she revealed herself. Once the mask was completely removed, it took every ounce of energy he had to try to maintain a neutral face.

Of course it's her. It had to be the world's idea of playing a cruel joke on him. Was she the worst date he'd ever had? Hell yeah. Was she still extremely beautiful? Absolutely. Did she still elicit feelings inside him that he wished would just go away? Of course she did. Was she the last person he wanted to see in his bedroom? Not really.

How, out of all the women in the world, was she the one standing in his bedroom wearing barely anything? Then she bit her lip, obvious desire in her gaze…and he lost his train of thought completely.

Chapter 2

Cover yourself, Winter thought to herself. She wanted to grab the blanket draped over the sofa so that Taheim would stop looking at her as though he wanted to cross the room and drag her to the bed. Even worse, she was sure she would willingly let him drag her anywhere.

She'd seen him at a couple events in Chicago since their blind date and had learned a bit more about him. But they had both managed to avoid each other most of the time, and when they didn't, they'd just ended up arguing about unrelated things. Even when they'd caught each other's gazes on occasion, it hadn't been anything like the sexual chemistry currently floating through the room.

"Kaya said I could come in here to change," she said nervously. She didn't even know why she was so nervous. One thing Winter didn't do was get nervous around men. Especially men she couldn't stand.

"No problem." She waited for him to say more, but his eyes trailed down to her body, reminding her that he had an unobstructed view of the most risqué part of the lingerie.

She quickly moved her hands to cover the front part of her thong and was rewarded by Taheim sucking in his breath in admiration.

"You look beautiful," he said as he brought his gaze back to her face. She blinked several times, caught off guard by his sincerity.

"Thanks."

"I just forgot something." He walked over to his dresser and pulled out what looked like a key. When he turned back to her, he didn't say anything.

She didn't know what was more awkward: the fact that he couldn't seem to find his voice after seeing her in little to no clothing, or the fact that she usually had a lot to say, but she, too, couldn't find the right words at the moment.

She was so caught up in her own thoughts that she didn't realize he was walking toward her until he was only a few inches away.

What is he up to? And why wasn't she backing away from him instead of moving closer?

When he reached her, he studied her eyes before his gaze dropped to her lips. She didn't want to mess up her lipstick, but she couldn't help but lick them. The groan that escaped his mouth made her bring her eyes toward his lips, as well. In her spare time, Winter often liked to paint, and the shape of his lips was the perfect subject.

Focus, Winter! Don't forget he was the worst blind date of your life. It wasn't that she'd forgotten that tidbit of info, but more like she was just choosing to ignore it.

"May I?" he asked, the deep timbre of his voice causing her nipples to harden instantly.

"Sure," she said, surprised that her voice was so breathless. *Wait, what did I just agree to?*

He must have sensed that she didn't know, because he smiled knowingly before kneeling to the floor.

Her eyes widened at the sight of him on his knees precisely adjacent to the part of her that was aching for his touch. *Dang!* The last touch she should be craving was his! A man who assumed that all he had to do was voice a few words and she'd turn to putty in his hand.

When his hands grazed her thighs, she shivered. She wasn't sure what he was doing and she was even more worried about the fact that deep down, she didn't care what he was doing.

She looked down at him and watched him study her left thigh-high. Strong fingers picked up the black ribbon on the thigh high, and slower than she liked, he tied a bow to match the one she'd made at the top of her right thigh.

When he stood back up, their eyes collided once again. The rise and fall of their chests moved in unison and the sexual tension caused her to shuffle from one heel to the other. The intensity in his stare was almost too much to handle.

"Winter, everyone's downstairs waiting for you to…"

They both turned toward the door as Danni entered and stopped midsentence.

"You're up," she finished as she looked from Winter to Taheim.

"I better go," he said as he turned and walked out the door.

"Um, any reason why you and the guy you claim to hate were in here looking as if you wanted to rip each other's clothes off?"

"Beats me." Winter shrugged. "I'm ready. Let's do this."

Danni was grinning like a kid on Christmas, which annoyed Winter even more. If she'd thought she didn't like Taheim before, she really couldn't stand him now.

There wasn't much that Winter Dupree couldn't handle, but she was certain that watching a roomful of women drool over Taheim Reed was a torture unlike anything she'd ever experienced.

"Did you hear the rumor that he has another clothing line in the works?" said a perky brunette to a couple women who had conveniently chosen to stand right in front of her and gawk at Taheim from afar. "I swear that man gets sexier by the day."

"Look at the way he moves across a room," said another woman. "I've heard the way he is in the bedroom is enough to keep a woman pining for more."

Taheim chose that exact moment to turn, giving them a nice view of his backside covered in a black sweater and dark jeans. "Oh man, I'd love to test-drive that," said the third woman.

Ugh, forget torture. Listening to them was enough to make her want to pop her eardrums. It wasn't that she particularly disagreed with them. Taheim was definitely sexy. Even she'd admit that. But unfortunately, his looks didn't mask the fact that he was still a jerk. A jerk that she had been fantasizing about ever since he'd walked in on her in his bedroom last week, wearing nothing but a babydoll and thong.

When Winter had accompanied her sister Autumn to a business convention in Chicago three years ago, they'd been convinced that the city was the perfect place to open their lingerie boutique, Bare Sophistication. Since their youngest sister, Summer, had a huge opportunity to work for a top New York fashion public relations firm, Winter and Autumn had agreed to take the reins and make the move to open their store. Living in New Jersey had been great, but she was glad she had a life in Chicago. Now, three years later, Winter didn't have any regrets except for one…going on a date with Taheim Reed.

Although she hadn't had any family in Chicago when she first moved, she hadn't been surprised when her cousins Micah and Malik Madden moved to the city from their respective towns. Micah had been a police officer in Arkansas before he joined forces with Shawn Miles to open M&M Security in Chicago. Malik, a private investigator with offices in Detroit and Chicago, had also decided to move from Detroit and make Chicago his permanent home. Why had both of her male cousins decided to move to Chi-Town? Well, as much as Winter and Autumn would have loved to believe a part of it had to do with them, Micah and Malik had both proved their moves had more to do with the Chicago natives they'd fallen in love with.

Which brought her to the reason she was attending this party despite the fact that it was being held at a lounge owned by Taheim's brother. She glanced over at the happy couples, who were beaming with joy. Her cousins had both fallen in love with cofounders of Elite

Events Incorporated, a very respected event-planning company headquartered in Chicago. Winter admired the success of the founders, Imani Rayne-Barker, Cydney Rayne-Miles, and Winter's cousin-in-law, Lexus Turner-Madden, and soon-to-be cousin-in-law, Mya Winters.

"I don't really understand the point of having engagement parties." Winter turned at the sound of her sister Autumn's voice.

Leave it to her sister to try to rationalize an event that people had been celebrating for decades. "You know, we should be happy that Micah married Lex and that Malik and Mya will be married soon. Especially since we and our other male cousins are nowhere close to getting married." Malik and Micah had four other brothers, all of whom were single. "And you should also prepare yourself for baby showers that I'm sure are right around the corner."

"Another pointless celebration," Autumn chimed in. "I'm happy for them. I just don't understand why we need manmade holidays, or in this case multiple celebrations, to celebrate a marriage. And baby showers are superficial. I curse the person who took such a sacred act as bringing a baby into the world and labeled the gathering a baby shower."

Winter gave her sister a blank stare. "Your brain never ceases to amaze me."

"What?" Autumn said with a shrug. "I thought you'd be happy that I came over to discuss my views on pointless celebrations rather than the fact that you obviously can't take your eyes off Taheim."

Her tone of voice was normal, but clearly, mentioning his name had gotten the attention of the women in front of them, who walked off after shooting them looks of irritation.

"See, and now you can thank me for running off those drooling women."

"Do you think before you speak?" Winter asked as she unscrewed her water bottle to take a much-needed sip. She refused to believe her sister was right, but deep down, she knew it was true. Looks-wise, Taheim Reed was everything she wanted in a man. His creamy milk-chocolate complexion, intense almost-black eyes and strong scored jawline had been the star of more than a few fantasies. Even worse, she'd even used him as inspiration when crafting a new lingerie line that she was working on for Bare Sophistication. Like her, he was also an entrepreneur, which she assumed was the only reason their mutual friends had thought they would be a good fit together.

She watched him walk over to his business partners for R&W Advertising, Jaleen Walker and Imani's husband, Daman Barker. That was another thing Winter hated that she liked about him. Whether it be women or men, people were just drawn to him. He was such a people person and his charismatic ways worked on everyone…except her. If they weren't arguing about the color of the sky, as if that even warranted an argument, they were pretending that the other person didn't exist. Her eyes roamed over his muscular arms encased in fabric before moving to the collared shirt peeking out from underneath his sweater. She appreciated his style and the fact that he always dressed to impress. Being that they were both designers, she understood making a fashion statement in clothing from your own line, but she'd bet that his athletic frame would look good in anything. Even better if he were wearing nothing at all.

Suddenly, her body tensed with awareness, causing her eyes to rush to his face. As she'd figured, his gaze was pinned to her, and for a brief second, she forgot that she hated the guy. That *he* was the worst blind date ever and the only guy she'd ever met who'd caused her to lose her temper in public. At the sound of her sister mumbling, she broke eye contact and turned to Autumn.

"Two forty-six, 247, 248, 249."

"Is there a reason you're counting?" Winter asked.

"Two fifty. As a matter of fact, there is a reason I was counting."

She waited for Autumn to continue and quickly realized that she wasn't going to explain further. She really wasn't surprised. Autumn spoke only when she felt it necessary or when she wanted to rattle off about a statistic or her point of view on certain topics. Her sister was the walking dictionary definition of brains and beauty. Winter could appreciate her uniqueness.

"And what reason were you counting, Autumn?"

"I was counting the number of seconds it took you to not so discreetly gape at Taheim. At thirty seconds your eyes showed interest. At 105 seconds you began to admire things about the way he looked tonight that I assume you hadn't allowed yourself to notice before. At 195 seconds your heart rate increased when you noticed he was staring at you just as intently. At 250 seconds you finally noticed I was counting."

She opened her mouth to say something about Autumn's observation but closed it when no words came out. She scrunched her eyes together instead before crossing her arms over her chest. A chill went down her spine when she thought about the fact that her sister's stats also meant that she and Taheim had spent almost a full minute just staring at each other.

"Don't give me that look," Autumn said. "Especially since you really aren't that upset at me, since your first coherent thought was obviously the fact that you and Taheim could spend that much time staring at each other. Pretty odd for enemies, don't you think?"

Winter finally let out a frustrated breath. "You don't know what I'm thinking." In response to Winter's statement, Autumn smiled. Truth be told, Winter and Autumn had been reading each other's minds since they were kids. When Summer felt left out, Winter had to remind her that she and Autumn were Irish twins since they were born eleven months apart.

"Whatever," she said with a wave of her hand. "He's easy on the eyes, so I just got a little distracted."

"Since your breathing still seems to be labored, I believe you meant to say that you got sexually aroused at the sight of him. Not distracted."

Winter uncrossed her hands and placed them on her hips. "For once, can you try not to state the obvious?"

"I didn't know I was stating the obvious," Autumn said in a serious tone. "I mean, I could tell you were sexually aroused and I wouldn't put it past a few others to notice the same chemistry whenever you both are in the same room. But I stated my observation because I didn't think it was obvious to you."

Winter dropped her hands to her sides and let out a deep sigh. She really didn't like the fact that Autumn was right yet again. She'd had no idea people could sense the sexual tension between her and Taheim.

"I'm stepping outside to get some air," she said as she pointed to the rooftop terrace. Maybe the cool late-October air would help lower her body temperature.

Chapter 3

"Taheim, did you hear what I said?"

Taheim tore his gaze away from the five-foot-seven cappuccino beauty with the luscious hips and round hazelnut-colored eyes in time to catch the intuitive glances of his friends Daman and Jaleen.

"Come again?" Taheim asked Daman. His friend shook his head.

"Never mind. It wasn't that important and I wouldn't want to stop you from watching Winter walk across the room."

"Man, I'm not even looking at that woman." Just as the words left his mouth, Winter glanced over her shoulder before stepping out onto the rooftop terrace. He instantly felt that familiar kick in his gut whenever she looked at him. That kick had gotten even stronger since he'd found her in his bedroom last week. Of all the women for him to be attracted to, it had to be the only woman in Chicago he didn't get along with.

"Oh really," Jaleen said, taking a swig of his beer. "So if your eyes weren't trained on Winter, who I must say is looking good tonight in that sleek black skirt and red blouse, then do tell who has your attention."

Taheim pinned Jaleen with an irritated stare before he quickly masked his feelings. He didn't like the fact that Jaleen sounded as if he was checking out Winter, even though he clearly didn't have any claims on her. In fact, his reaction was downright ridiculous considering his nonexistent relationship, and friendship, with Winter.

"With all the sexy single ladies in this room, Winter Dupree is definitely not getting my attention." He waved his arms around the room to emphasize his point.

Daman and Jaleen shared a look of disbelief that didn't go unnoticed by Taheim.

"Seriously, guys, that's a headache I don't need right now."

"Problems with your clothing line?"

"No, sales are great and I even have a big city tour scheduled for next spring to visit the retail stores that will start carrying the line next year."

"Then what's the problem?"

Taheim took a sip of his tequila. "It's the men's nightwear line that I want to debut before the end of the year. I'd like to get it in stores early next year and talk to retailers about it during the big city tour. T.R. Night will be different from the clothing line, and I guess I'm just trying to figure out the perfect time for a debut."

"If you're worried about the market accepting T.R. Night like they did Collegiate Life, then I don't think you have anything to worry about. The release will be successful."

He nodded his head at Daman, glad that he had friends who knew just what to say when it came to his diving into another project. Taheim was an entrepreneur in every sense of the word. In addition to being a cofounder of R&W Advertising and the creator of Collegiate Life, he handled all the marketing, promotions and advertising for his brother's chain of nightclubs and lounges, as well as his parents' Midwest restaurant chain. Even with all his success, every now and then he ventured into a project more personal than the others. In this case, T.R. Night was that project.

"Thanks, man. The nightwear line has been a little more challenging than the clothing line, but I'm really excited about this."

"You should be," Jaleen said. "And if you're stuck on any designs, there is this one designer who specializes in nightwear who I'm sure could offer you some great ideas."

"In Chicago? I'm pretty familiar with all the designers in the city. Besides, I think I'm okay on the designs." There were a few things he questioned, but for the most part, he knew he would figure it out.

"I was referring to Winter."

Taheim shot Jaleen a look of disbelief. "Is there a reason you keep bringing her up today?"

"I'm just saying. She's got talent and if you are struggling with any designs, she could probably help."

"I don't and never will need the help of Winter Dupree. We can barely stand being in the same room with one another, let alone discuss business. I'll pass on that."

Jaleen shrugged. "So did you decide on a date for the debut?"

"I actually have a meeting tomorrow morning with Ajay to discuss something he had in mind for the grand opening of his night lounge in December." His brother had worked hard to be the most successful club and lounge owner in Chicago and Taheim was glad to see he was finally reaping the benefits of all his hard work.

He was about to continue when he felt a jolt in his pants. *Crap.* He already knew that Winter had returned from the rooftop terrace without even turning in her direction.

Don't look her way, he thought to himself. It wasn't that he cared what his friends would think if they caught him staring at her again, but rather the fact that he needed to get through the rest of the night without imagining her in that mouthwatering lingerie.

Despite his best efforts, his head slowly turned to where she had joined her sister. He hated to admit it, but he was still disappointed by the way he had acted during their blind date. Yes, there were times that he went into dates already knowing that they would end with the woman in his bed, but he hadn't gone into his date with Winter assuming that. But the minute he'd seen her sitting there her beauty had taken him aback. Winter wasn't the type of woman to cake on too much makeup every day, but rather she applied just the right amount to accentuate her features.

When women met him, they immediately wanted to date him. Unfortunately, it wasn't only because of his looks and personality but also because of his money. Or the money they assumed he would dish out to them. Sometimes he felt like a walking ATM rather than an astute businessman who had been fortunate enough to land a few successful business deals. Winter didn't seem like other women, and instead of going into the date differently, he'd acted like a jerk.

He watched her bring her water bottle to her mouth, instantly jealous of the item as her lips closed around the rim. Lips that would look perfect enclosed around his mouth instead. His eyes left her lips and connected with hers, and he was not surprised to see her looking back at him. He thought she shot him a soft smile, but he was too far across the room to tell.

"So this is you paying attention to other women and ignoring Winter?" Jaleen asked, as he looked in Taheim's line of vision.

"Whatever, man."

"Why don't you just ask her out again?" Daman asked.

"Hell naw, I can't. The last one was bad enough."

Daman and Jaleen shared a look, but luckily, they changed the subject. He was being serious when he said he couldn't ask her out again; however, the reason why wasn't that the last one had been so bad. The real reason he couldn't ask her out again was because deep down, he feared what would happen if the date actually went well.

Taheim admired the exterior of the lounge that his brother Ajay was opening in a month and a half. The South Loop area in Chicago had a good vibe to it and he had every idea the lounge would be successful.

"Ajay, you in here?" he yelled as he walked through the side door.

"I'm back here, bro."

He followed the sound of his brother's voice until he reached a room in the back of the lounge.

"What's up," Ajay said as they touched fists. "How was Malik and Mya's engagement party yesterday? I hate that I missed it, but this place keeps me busy."

"It was nice. The team you have working there was great."

"That's why I will be intermixing that staff with the new staff I hire for this location. I want Inferno Lounge to be the best in the city."

"Well, it's definitely the largest," he said as he thought about how massive the venue was when he entered.

"Thanks." Ajay moved a few boxes off his desk and desk chair before pulling out two chairs from a closet.

"Why did you pull out an extra chair?"

Just as Ajay was about to answer, he was cut off by a female voice. "Hello, is anyone here?"

"One sec, bro," Ajay said as he left to get the woman behind the voice. As he listened to his brother greet the woman, he strained to make out the details of her voice. It was soft but slightly husky at the same time. It was the type of voice that would be perfect for one of those naughty call centers.

The closer they got, the more aware Taheim's body became. If he wasn't mistaken, the voice sounded a lot like…

"Taheim, I hope you don't mind but I asked Winter Dupree from Bare Sophistication to join our meeting."

From the stunned look on her face, he assumed she was just as surprised to see him.

"I don't mind," he said. When Ajay motioned for her to sit in the chair next to Taheim and their arms brushed, he immediately regretted the words that had just come out of his mouth. He should have told his brother that he definitely did mind and that he would prefer he discuss their business before he discussed whatever business he had with Winter. Which begged the question, *What business does my brother have with Winter?*

He brushed off the same jealousy he'd felt when Jaleen had complimented the way Winter looked yesterday.

"So, as you both know, Inferno will be opening the week before Christmas. I've been racking my brain about the type of grand opening I want to have and I've decided that a masquerade gala would be the perfect event."

"That's a great idea," Taheim said as Winter expressed similar sentiments.

"Thanks, guys. So that means this event has to be the best lounge event Chicagoans have ever seen." He took out a couple sheets of paper and handed a sheet to each of them. "I ran my idea by Elite Events since they will be planning the majority of the grand opening, including a huge part that will require the expertise of both of you."

Winter looked up from the paper. "And what might that be?"

"On the back side of that sheet, you will see the details of the masquerade lingerie fashion show I want to be the central feature of the grand opening."

Taheim scanned the back side of the paper and assumed that Winter was doing the same.

"I'm confused, Ajay," Taheim said. "So you want Winter and me to plan the fashion show?"

"Yes. You both have done fashion shows before and Elite Events has a lot of other items to work on for the grand opening. Winter, I heard that you were working on a new line for the holidays that will release next week or so, correct?"

"That's right. Some pieces are out already."

"And, Taheim, you need to debut T.R. Night before you go on tour next spring, right? What about creating some holiday nightwear and, of course, you could show some pieces from the Collegiate line, as well."

He chanced a glance at Winter, who didn't seem any more thrilled by the idea than he was.

"Listen," Ajay said as he waved his hand at both of them. "I know you both have heard that the Department of Cultural Affairs and Special Events is trying their best to make Chicago a fashion-forward city and that includes more fashion-focused events. It's a great opportunity to showcase your work and it would really help me out a lot."

Taheim ran his fingers across his face. There was nothing he wouldn't do for his family and Ajay knew that.

"Of course I'll do it, bro."

"Thanks, man." Taheim and Ajay both looked at Winter.

"I'm in, too," she said hesitantly. "It sounds like fun."

"Great! So I suggest you both share contact info and start planning this fashion show. There are some organizations that I've partnered with who may have opportunities for you both to showcase some work, as well, but I'll let you both know as those opportunities arise. I'm really excited to bring a holiday collection from Bare Sophistication and T.R. Night to Chicago. I'll leave you both to discuss the best way to begin planning. Remember, Elite Events is here to help, too."

Yeah, right! It was his friends at Elite Events who had gotten him into this mess with Winter in the first place. First the blind date and now planning a fashion show together? Ajay had always been a forward thinker, but he wasn't a schemer. This had Elite Events written all over it.

He glanced over at Winter, taking note that she still hadn't looked him in the eye. He ran his hand over his forehead before placing his forearms on his thighs, trying to think of what to say. In all his thirty-three years, he'd never been at a loss for words around a woman. "I guess we need to set up a date to meet. What day works for you next week?"

She didn't turn to look at him right away, but when she did, she looked as though she'd rather have been doing anything else than having this conversation.

"Look," he said, clasping his hands together. "I don't like this idea any more than you do. But I would love the exposure and I'm sure you would, too. And since Ajay's my brother, I couldn't say no even if I wanted to."

"But that's insane."

"What is?"

"What's insane is the fact that your brother or anyone else would think we could work well together. Over the past couple months, every time we talk, it turns into a debate or an argument. You and I don't get along." She waved her hand between the two of them.

"That's because you disagree with everything I say."

She gave him the side-eye. "Actually, you are the one who starts most of the arguments."

"No, I don't," he said as he turned his chair more to face her. "Just last month at that fund-raising event that you and I both attended where we happened to be placed at the same table, I was talking to that high school principal about the benefit of a growing man having a good male role model to look up to."

"And I didn't disagree," Winter interjected. "In fact, I agreed with you. I was just pointing out that the same goes for a woman having a good female role model. Sometimes I feel like women get left out of the equation. We need positive role models just like men."

"But that wasn't the conversation. That principal was talking about the program he'd created at his school for young men."

"Exactly my point," Winter said, turning her chair, as well. "Why start a program for the male students and not have one for the female students? Why segregate the programs at all?"

"I never said I disagreed with you either. I just pointed out the fact that that wasn't the current topic of discussion."

"Yeah, and you pointed it out in front of the eight other people at the table, who laughed and then disregarded my suggestion."

He placed his hands on his chest. "So you're mad that they thought I was funny?"

She lifted her eyebrows. "How in the world do you

process information? It wasn't because they thought you were funny. It was because they lost sight of my point."

"Because they were only focused on laughing at me and talking about my viewpoint?"

"Once again, you somehow made this about you." She sighed and closed her eyes, the sound distracting him from listening to whatever else was coming out of her mouth.

"Taheim, did you hear anything I just said?"

"Every word," he said as his eyes dropped to her lips. She must have noticed the change in his mood, because her lips parted with awareness.

"So," Ajay said, reentering the room and breaking the trance between him and Winter. "Did you guys settle when you'd have your first meeting?"

Winter stood and put back on her coat. "Your brother is the most difficult human being to ever walk the planet."

Ajay laughed as he looked from Winter to Taheim. "Tell me something I don't know."

"Call me at Bare Sophistication when you're ready to set up a meeting," she said to Taheim as she left the office.

"She was in a hurry," Ajay said as he sat back in his desk chair. "What did you say to her? Because clearly, it was the wrong thing to say."

He glanced at the seat that Winter had just vacated. "When it comes to that woman, what don't I say that's wrong?"

Chapter 4

Winter's navy heels clicked on the wood surface in a tempo that matched the hard sound of the rain pounding on the window. It seemed fitting that an early-November rainstorm paired perfectly with her sour mood. A mood that had been one of many ever since she'd heard the news about working with Taheim on the fashion show a couple days ago.

It was a great opportunity, but no matter how hard she tried, she couldn't slow her heart rate whenever she thought about working closely with him. She glanced over at an unfinished lace cami that she wasn't sure she could even complete today, as planned. Her creativity was even starting to suffer because her mind was working overtime trying to figure out how she would handle the situation with Taheim.

Autumn appeared at the door. "Can you please stop

pacing? I can hear your footsteps down the hall and you're giving me a headache."

She ignored her sister's comment since evidently, she had no idea how much anxiety she was experiencing. Winter *never* got anxious about anything, but the end of the year was bringing on quite a few behavioral changes for her.

"You're the one who came back here to my design studio."

"Aren't we testy this evening," Autumn said as she walked farther into the room. "But seriously, you're going to put a hole in the floor."

"I'll stop pacing as soon as I figure out how to work with Taheim without losing my sanity."

"I've never seen you like this. He must be getting under your skin more than I had initially thought."

Winter stopped pacing and turned to face Autumn. "He doesn't get under my skin. He's more like that irritating itch that no matter how much you scratch, it still itches."

"How is that any different from what I said?"

"You made it seem like I allow him to bother me more than I've ever let any man bother me before."

Autumn walked over to Winter and placed an arm on her shoulder, which was covered in a navy jacket that went perfectly with her white top and dark jeans.

"Oh, I'm sorry," Autumn replied. "I meant to indicate that he gets to you more than *anyone* has in the past. Male or female."

Winter rolled her eyes before walking over to the massive wooden table currently covered in red, silver and black fabrics. "Is there a reason you're here?

I thought you had to help Danni change the fixtures in the store."

"I do, but I got distracted by this guy asking me if he could discuss business with you. Something about some new design ideas, I think. I'm not sure."

"Okay, I'll meet with him real quick." It wasn't as if she were getting much work done anyway. Usually on Friday evening after the busy lunch crowd, Winter enjoyed spending time cooped up in her studio turning her creative ideas into a reality. Today she'd barely gotten anything done, so maybe talking to someone about possible business would be enough to jump-start her creative juices.

"Where is he?" she asked as she stepped into the store.

"He's over there." She followed the direction of Autumn's hand and immediately shot her sister a look of irritation.

"Are you kidding me? You made it seem like it was a person I didn't know."

Autumn smirked. "I never said you didn't know him. I only said it was a guy who was distracting me. In this case, that person is Taheim, but what does it matter? You said he doesn't affect you any more than anyone else."

Instead of responding to Autumn, she stood there and stared at her sister in silence.

"You can stare me down all you want, but that won't change the fact that Taheim is waiting to talk to you. Sixty percent of the population lie to themselves in hopes of believing that lie."

Winter squinted her eyes together. "And you're telling me this in order to say what exactly?"

"That the sooner you stop lying to yourself about the way Taheim affects you, the quicker you can figure out how to handle the situation."

"I don't even know why I asked," Winter said, throwing up her hands in defeat.

"I do," Autumn said with a shrug. "You're delaying seeing Taheim. But time is up and the store is slow now, so Danni and I have to change those fixtures. Why don't you take him to your office or studio?"

Not that she had a choice, since Autumn was already ushering her to Taheim. She didn't particularly like the fact that he had dropped by without even calling the store and asking her if it was okay. *That's because he's used to doing whatever he wants.* It wasn't that she had been waiting on his call. But since they really did have business to discuss, she'd figured he would have actually scheduled a meeting with her.

As she got closer to him, she tried to ignore her nerves. Her palms were growing sweatier by the second. The last time that had happened was her senior year at the New York School of Design when she had to present her final design to the board before graduating. And even with that situation, she wasn't sure the circumstances compared. *This is ridiculous on so many levels.* Fast heartbeat. Sweaty palms. Moist thighs. *What in the world is wrong with me?*

Crap. All those reactions represented those of a woman who was attracted to a man. *No shit, Sherlock, you are attracted to him.* But being attracted to him and acting on that attraction were two different things.

"Hi, Taheim. Did you stop by to talk business?" *Way to go, Dupree.* Had she really just alluded to the fact that he would stop by to discuss anything other than business?

He turned around slowly in a way that made her wonder if he had to brace himself before seeing her. When his eyes landed on hers, it took all her strength not to gasp aloud. He placed his hands in the pockets of his black pea coat and she tried not to look down at the zipper of his jeans, which was now exposed.

Ever since he had found her in his bedroom, she'd replayed every minute of the encounter and wondered if he would ever look at her the way he'd looked at her that night.

"Hello, Winter." He gave her a quick once-over. If she had blinked, she would have missed it. "Yes, I was hoping now was a good time. But if it isn't, we can schedule something else."

"No, this is fine. How about we head to my design studio."

The short walk to her studio was filled with awareness of him and she wished he didn't have to smell so good. *Hmm, I wonder what cologne he's wearing*, she thought as she remembered that day in his bedroom. *Maybe it's the Kenneth Cole.*

When she walked into her studio, she motioned for him to enter. He lightly brushed past her, filling her senses even more. *Or maybe it's whatever was in that silver bottle.* Regardless of what cologne he was wearing, it was driving her crazy. The type of crazy that made a woman want to place tender kisses all over a man's neck and get lost in his scent.

He stopped in the middle of her studio and did a three-hundred-sixty-degree turn. "You have a nice studio. I bet you create lots of lingerie pieces in here."

She started to tidy up her wooden design table before she remembered that she liked it messy. "Thanks. Usually I have about two or three pieces created by this time today."

He nodded his head slightly to the side as he observed some strips of silver satin that were lying across the corner of the table. "By the tone of your voice, I assume you haven't accomplished as much as you need to accomplish for the day."

"I guess you could say that," she said with a slight laugh.

Watching him walk around her studio was a little unnerving. Although she had decided to meet in her studio instead of her office, she felt as though he was invading her space. When he turned his back to observe the framed pictures of fabric that filled her walls, she couldn't help but check out his butt.

Good Lawd. Firm. Round. Squeezable. She had no idea why, but she'd always had a thing for a man's butt. When she was in college, she had dated this rock singer she'd met when he'd pulled her from the audience and brought her onstage. She didn't particularly care to listen to rock music all the time, but every now and then she liked to hit up bars and watch a live performance.

They'd dated for a couple months and always seemed to have sex in the most unconventional places. Backstage against a wall… In his dressing rooms… Or her favorite, under the stage when another band performed. The vibrations she'd felt during those explosive moments were indescribable. Then one day, they'd finally had sex in her apartment and she'd taken one look at his butt and known they had to break up. It was so flat she swore it caved in.

Taheim bent over to look at her bookcase filled with fabric and design books. *Oh yeah, underneath those jeans is definitely an ass I'd love to get my hands on.*

"Are you finished?"

Winter jumped at the sound of his voice and placed her hand over her heart.

"Yes, I'm done." What was she supposed to say? There was no use denying that she had been checking him out. She'd been so busy staring at his backside she hadn't expected to catch him looking over his shoulder at her.

"Why haven't you been inspired today?" he asked as he leaned against the table and crossed his arms over his chest. She wasn't used to this Taheim. They had been together for more than ten minutes and an argument hadn't broke out yet. *That's because you could cut this sexual tension with a knife. But you CAN'T. GO. THERE.* Why, oh why, was her body not listening to what her mind was telling her?

"I don't know," she finally said with a shrug. "The part of my brain directly connected to my inspiration must be clogged tonight."

Maybe if I start talking about my ideas for the fashion show, we can get down to business. Although it would be so much easier if he didn't look so sexy leaning up against the table. But at the end of the day, he was just a man. A man who had annoyed her more than any man she'd ever met. She would have to be professional around him, ignore her attraction to him and definitely ignore the butterflies swarming around in her stomach.

His mouth lifted in a side smile that she wished didn't look so suggestive. "Maybe I can help unclog your inspiration."

Crap. So much for ignoring the butterflies.

What are you doing, man? he asked himself. This was the complete opposite of ignoring his attraction to Winter.

When he'd gotten into his car after leaving his firm, he hadn't noticed that he wasn't headed home until he was parking down the street from Bare Sophistication.

The lack of parking in front of the store should have been enough to make him turn around and go home. And when he didn't see Winter through the store window, he really should have brought his ass home. But then he remembered that every time he walked into his bedroom, he thought about Winter. Next thing he knew, he was walking into her store asking for her.

From the look on her face right now, he could tell that his statement intrigued her. He openly looked her up and down. The way she was wearing those navy heels was making it hard for him to remember to be a gentleman. Navy was his favorite color. Always had been. When his eyes made their way to her breasts, he had to remind himself that he had just decided to be a gentleman moments prior. But his eyes had a mind of their own and the way her nipples peaked beneath her white shirt made it hard for him to tear his gaze away.

"Are you finished?" she asked, throwing his words back at him.

"What's wrong?" he asked as he lifted his hands in an innocent gesture. "I saw more than just your nipples hardening that night I caught you in my bedroom."

Her eyes squinted together and Taheim swore he could see the heat seeping off her neck in frustration.

She lifted her hands to the ceiling. "Thank you for reminding me why I dislike you so much."

She walked closer to him and looked him dead in the eye. "For a minute, I forgot the cocky jerk you are."

He welcomed her change in attitude because he wasn't too keen on the direction his thoughts were headed. Now that they had to work together, he really needed to find a way to ignore his attraction to her.

"How about we exchange the ideas we've had for the fashion show so far."

She squinted her eyes together as if trying to gauge if he was serious. "Okay," she finally said. "We can sit over here."

He followed her to a set of matching teal chairs that had a black coffee table in between them.

"So, I thought about what your brother said about the masquerade gala, and since masquerade lingerie fashion shows are kinda my thing, I already know the perfect place to get winter-wonderland masks for the models. Also, I've already spoken to Elite Events and gotten the details on how they are decorating Inferno for the gala."

"Perfect." He pulled out his small notebook from his pocket to review the notes he'd written. "I met with Ajay this morning, and he wants us each to show at least ten pieces. But I'm also showing about five or six pieces from Collegiate Life, so if you want to show five extra lingerie pieces from your other collection, Ajay said that'd be cool."

"I can definitely do that," Winter said as she clasped her hands together. "How about I pick pieces that coincide with the Collegiate Life pieces you choose so that everything will be cohesive."

"I like that. I think it would be great if we have at least 30 models. Fifteen men and fifteen women."

"I'll start composing the language for a model search," Winter said as she stood to get her notebook off the wooden table.

They discussed several more ideas and Taheim was surprised that they seemed to be on the same page with the way they wanted the fashion show to go. But there was still a lot more planning to do and only time would tell if their ideas continued to complement each other.

Chapter 5

Taheim grabbed the medium-sized basketball from under his glass desk and tossed it in the air. Tossing the ball around had always helped him clear his mind. He wasn't sure when he started finding the act so therapeutic, but lately it seemed he couldn't shuffle through his thoughts without it.

It had been four days since he'd discussed business with Winter and it seemed he couldn't stop thinking about her. It wasn't just because his attraction to her seemed to grow every time they were in the same room. It actually had a lot to do with the reoccurring dream he'd had about debuting his new line. Usually his creative ideas were flowing, but lately he'd felt stuck.

T.R. Night was supposed to be the nightwear collection that redefined the type of clothing men should sleep in. He wanted to be the designer that everyone had been labeling him to be since he'd released Collegiate Life. But nightwear wasn't the same as apparel. Although it might seem as if lounge pants, boxers and V-neck shirts were simple to design, he needed to create designs that represented T.R. Night to the fullest. And the pieces he'd been staring at in his condo that morning definitely weren't it.

You should just ask her for her design expertise. He'd had that thought more than once, but every time he glanced at his phone to give her a call, he remembered that he had something to prove. She thought he was just an egotistical jerk, and although a part of her belief might have been right, based off how he'd treated her on their blind date, that wasn't the way he wanted her to see him.

But there is nothing wrong with asking for help when you need it, right?

His smartphone chimed, jarring him from his thoughts. He tucked the basketball under his arm and glanced at the screen. His eyes squinted in surprise as he answered.

"Hey, Winter."

"Hey, Taheim, are you free to chat?"

"Sure, what's up?"

"Well, since the fashion show is six weeks away, we really need to solidify the models. So I was thinking that we should probably hold a casting call this Saturday."

He leaned up in his chair. "That soon? That's four days away."

"Yeah, are you free?"

"I can be."

"Great! I have a lot of contacts in the industry and on social media, so I'll send something out. I already talked to your brother and he said he's fine with us having the models audition at Inferno Saturday afternoon. If it's not a success, we'll plan a second model call, but I have a feeling we'll have no problem finding all the models we need."

"That's good. I'll send something out on social media, as well. Do you want to text me what wordage you're using? Or better yet, I can text you what I think we can use on Twitter and Facebook and you tell me if you're okay with the message."

"Hmm, I'm better with concise words, so maybe you should come up with the Facebook messaging and I should come up with the Twitter messaging."

He smiled into the phone. "Is that a challenge I hear in your voice?"

"Not a challenge," she said with a laugh. "More like an observation."

"Have you forgotten what I do for a living?" he asked, referring to R&W Advertising. "Marketing and advertising are kinda my thing."

"Well, fashion shows and models are kinda my thing."

There was nothing that thrilled Taheim more than being underestimated. "Tell you what," he said as an idea suddenly popped into his head. "How about you and I both create targeted messaging for the model call and we post the info on all our social media pages. Every model who comes to the call must state where they heard about it and we'll track our retweets, comments and likes to see who gets more hits. My company specializes in tracking social media campaigns, so this will be a breeze."

The other line grew quiet, and for a second, he thought she'd decline his challenge.

"You're on," she said confidently. "And to up the ante, the loser has to be the other's bitch for a week."

"Say what?" Taheim glanced at his phone as if he'd heard her wrong. "And what exactly would that include? Because my mind is already thinking of things I need you to do." He was sure her idea and his idea were completely opposite. Her thoughts probably involved him cooking her dinner or bringing her coffee, and while his ideas included those same duties, he'd be adding a few more not-so-innocent things to that list.

"First off, get your mind out of the gutter. I'm talking about bringing the other one coffee and picking up their clothes from the cleaner's. Maybe bringing them lunch on days we have practice for the fashion show. Those sorts of things."

"Chicken," he said, still smiling. "You're on. I never back down from a challenge."

After they hung up, he still had a smile on his face. *What the heck is wrong with me?* He wasn't the type to smile after hanging up with a woman and he definitely didn't want to think about how much he had been smiling when they were on the phone.

"Man, why the hell do you have that stupid smile on your face?"

Taheim looked up to find Jaleen in the doorway.

"It's nothing. Just got some good news about the city tour for Collegiate Life in the spring."

Jaleen looked at him suspiciously. "Naw, man,

I know that look. You must have been talking to a woman."

Taheim stood from his desk and continued throwing the basketball into the air. "Why are you all in my business?"

"Can't a friend just be concerned?"

Taheim stopped throwing the ball. "Is there something I can help you with?"

Jaleen laughed as he plopped down in a chair. "Actually, I came in here because I overheard you on the phone when I was passing in the hallway. You were talking to Winter, right?"

"Yeah, it was her. We had to discuss some plans for that fashion show I was telling you about." Taheim sat back in his desk chair and waited for Jaleen to mock him. He'd been teasing him about Winter for months, so he was ready for a jab or two.

"From what I heard, you two placed a bet on who could get the most models to your first model call, right?"

"You really need to let private conversations remain private."

"Next time, you should shut your door." Jaleen lifted his left foot and bent it over his right knee. "And I hope you know that you have to win this. It would look bad if the cofounder of a firm that specializes in advertising and marketing lost."

Taheim gave him a look of disbelief. "Man, I got this. You know I've got the social media game on lock. Besides, Winter has only been in Chicago for a couple years and I spent my entire life here. She may have a lot of connections outside Illinois, but I'm sure my Chicago connections will help spread the word to more models."

"Are you sure about that?" Jaleen said, giving him a sly smile.

"Yeah, I'm sure," he said hesitantly. He never did like when Jaleen looked at him that way.

"I wouldn't underestimate Winter," Jaleen said as he pulled his smartphone out of his pocket and tapped a few buttons before giving Taheim his phone. "Just like you, she aims to win."

Taheim shook his head as he read aloud the Twitter message that Winter had sent. "'They can imitate your style, but not your walk. Calling all models. Saturday @ 1pm @ Inferno. Be there. #InfernoChicago #LingerieFashionShow.'"

Damn. She wasted no time. "She must have put this up right after we hung up."

"Nope," Jaleen said as he took back his phone. "Like I said, I was outside the door, so I looked at her page right after y'all made the bet. She was probably typing as you were talking. She already has thirty retweets and it's only been a couple of minutes."

"So that's how she wants to play," he said as he picked up his phone, which he'd placed on his desk.

He began typing his tweet.

Blurring the lines between reality & fantasy. Join our fantasy. Model call. Inferno. Saturday @ 1pm. #CollegiateLife #TRNight #InfernoChicago

"There we go," Taheim said as he sat back and watched the retweets trickle in.

* * *

"Oh, he's good," Winter told Autumn as she watched the number of retweets rise on Taheim's tweet.

"Is he getting more retweets than you?"

"Crap, I see why. I forgot to hashtag Bare Sophistication. He hashtagged both of his clothing lines."

"Well, then, post another tweet. I know you want to win and I'm competitive, too. Your first tweet was inspiring and I liked it. But now you need to hit back harder."

As Autumn went to help a customer who had entered their store, Winter's lips quirked to the side in thought. *How can I allude to the fact that one-of-a-kind Bare Sophistication pieces will be shown at this fashion show?* She needed something catchy. Something that would make women swoon and men drool.

Her fingers began typing, and when they stopped moving, she smiled in satisfaction at accomplishing her goal.

"Did you come up with something?" Autumn asked as she walked back over to the checkout counter. Instead of responding, Winter handed Autumn her phone.

Autumn read the tweet aloud. "'Exclusive. Chic. Delicious. Do you have what it takes to bare your sophistication? Saturday 1pm. Model call. #InfernoChicago #BareSophistication.'"

Autumn nodded her head before speaking. "That's perfect," she said before going back to tend to customers.

Within minutes, she already had double the amount of retweets she'd had before. Then she remembered that she hadn't written anything on her Facebook or Instagram pages and immediately wrote similar statements on both pages and accompanied the messages with an image that they'd taken for Bare Sophistication's website.

Her phone dinged, signaling that she had a notification on Twitter. It took all her energy not to grind her teeth together in frustration when she saw Taheim's latest tweet.

@TRNight + @BareSophistication = explosive chemistry. Model call @InfernoChicago. Sat. 1pm. Rip the runway this winter.

"Ugh," Winter said aloud in frustration. She'd been really trying to beat Taheim to the punch and tweet about both of their lines before he got the chance to do so. When Danni got back from lunch, she left the counter and walked around the store to get inspiration for her next tweet.

She didn't care that Taheim was great at marketing and developing taglines. She still wanted to win the bet. She bit her bottom lip as she went to the far right of the store, where they featured pieces from their holiday collection.

She ran her fingers over the delicate red, silver, black and pink garments, paying extra-close attention to the seductive pink skirt and midriff halter trimmed in white fur. The piece was called Santa's Little Helper and they recommended that customers pair it with their candy-cane thigh-highs.

Just like that, she was inspired for her next tweet.

Are you on Santa's naughty list? Changing the face of lingerie/nightwear. Get caught on the runway @InfernoChicago @BareSophistication @TRNight

She didn't have enough characters to add the day and time of the model call, but she expanded her message on her other social media sites and paired it with an image of the Santa's Little Helper piece. Just like with the other messages and tweets, she received retweets, comments and likes within minutes.

She strode to her design studio with extra pep in her step. When she'd called Taheim an hour or so prior, her only intention had been to tell him that they needed to have a model call that weekend. She really hadn't expected them to get into a Twitter war.

She slowed her stride as she walked over to a chair in her studio. She hadn't looked in a mirror, but she could feel herself smiling widely and it wasn't just because Taheim hadn't tweeted in the past few minutes. She was cheesing extra hard just at the thought of him, which didn't make any sense. Yeah, they had been getting along recently, but she couldn't allow herself to forget how they'd first met. Thinking of him as Taheim the arrogant jerk was a helluva lot easier than thinking of him as Taheim the sexy charmer whose deep voice often lured her to sleep, resulting in the most seductive fantasies she'd ever had in her life.

As she sat down, her phone dinged and she noticed it was a text message from Taheim.

So since we're changing the face of lingerie and nightwear, are we on this so-called naughty list?

She smiled, *again*, before responding.

I guess you can say that. To get everyone to indulge in this masquerade lingerie fashion show, I'd say we all have to get a little naughty, don't you think?

As she was texting Taheim back, another tweet sparked in her mind, so she typed the tweet as quickly as she could.

Masquerade + holiday lingerie = a winter wonderland to remember. Dare to indulge. Model call 1pm @InfernoChicago. #BareSophistication #TRNight

Right after she hit Enter on the tweet, she received another text message from Taheim.

Sneaky, but I like it.

Her heart began beating fast, as if he were voicing the words to her in person rather than text message. She wished such simple words didn't amuse her, but they did.

@WinterDupree designs are what all MY dreams are made of. See what happens when visions collide for the holidays. @TRNight @InfernoChicago

She was just about to text him when he entered another tweet.

They said one day I'd meet my match. Knew it was true the day I saw her in those black stilettos. @WinterDupree @InfernoChicago #Modelcall1pm

"Oh, goodness," she said to herself as her breath caught in her throat. The only day he'd seen her in black stilettos was the day he'd caught her in his bedroom. They hadn't really talked about it, and of course none of their followers knew what he was referring to, with the exception of Danni, who'd walked in on them, and her sister Autumn, whom she'd told. But his tweet felt personal. As if he was telling the world just how much that day had affected him.

Since they were both planning the fashion show, any indication that there was more going on between them than just fashion would make people talk. As predicted, his tweet began getting retweets and comments started rolling in asking if the two of them were dating.

She texted him and added an emoji of a face that was not pleased. In fact, the emoji was giving him the side-eye and a frown.

You're a flirt and you're playing dirty.

She watched the little dots on her iPhone screen appear, indicating that he was replying.

Who said I was playing.

It was quickly followed up by an emoji similar to the one she had sent, but instead of a frown, it was giving a side smile. Before she could contemplate his words, another text message came through.

That's the only day I can ever recall being speech-less. Then again, I'm not sure what guy could find you standing in his bedroom wearing that outfit and not lose his train of thought and ability to speak. You looked beautiful.

She stared at her phone, unsure if she should respond to his text. Then she remembered that she'd always been a bold person who expressed how she felt, so she didn't see why this moment should be any different.

She started typing her response.

The way you stared at me that night made me feel beautiful. You seemed genuine and approachable despite the situation.

She glanced to the side and smiled before writing the rest of her response and pressing Send.

You're still cocky as hell. But underneath all that is a man with a story. Hopefully I'll hear it one day.

Chapter 6

"For those of you who don't know, Inferno Lounge is opening the second Saturday in December, so this fashion show is in five weeks. We have a lot to pull together in a short amount of time. If you can't keep up with the pace or have too many holiday obligations, you will be cut."

Taheim looked toward the slew of model hopefuls, observing the way that Winter commanded the room. It was hard to keep his eyes off her, and judging from the way she had the attention of most of the men in the room, he wasn't the only one who was under her spell.

"As much as we'd love to have each of you in the fashion show, we aren't able to hire everyone."

The social media battle between him and Winter had brought on the largest model call that he'd ever seen. Winter had looped in the help of her Bare

Sophistication staff, who had assisted with fashion shows she'd had, and he'd recruited the help of his Collegiate Life team, who specialized in fashion shows, as well. Together they had pulled enough resources and contacts to assemble a great team to plan the fashion show. This gave Elite Events the opportunity to focus on planning the masquerade gala.

Winter glanced over at him and nodded her head for him to pick up the conversation where she'd left off.

"Out of two hundred hopefuls that arrived Saturday at 1:00 p.m., you were the top forty-five. We appreciate each of you for coming out this Monday evening, but we only need thirty to thirty-five models. So a few of you won't make it."

He leaned up from the back wall and went to stand beside Winter. "This masquerade gala will be the talk of the town and Inferno is already being predicted as one of the best lounge and club debuts to hit the Chicago scene in decades. Thanksgiving is only a couple weeks away and Christmas is right after, so as Winter stated, we won't have time for excuses that you have too much going on for the holidays. Remember, there is someone eager to take your spot."

"You aren't just representing yourself and Inferno in this fashion show," Winter said to the group. "Taheim and I are both debuting pieces from our collections, so you're representing Bare Sophistication, T.R. Night and Collegiate Life, as well."

Taheim inwardly smiled at the excited looks he witnessed on most of the models' faces. "I'm also going on a city tour early next year for Collegiate Life and T.R. Night. I have a few openings for a couple male and female models who wouldn't mind joining to wear my clothing for some of the biggest urban retailers in the country." A few guys clapped hands and a few of the ladies squealed.

"And, ladies, for you there is even more opportunity," Winter said, clasping her hands together. "Word has spread that Bare Sophistication's masquerade lingerie events are the most exclusive events to hit the private party scene in years. We will be expanding that business next year to more cities, starting with places in the Midwest. I'll need to have reliable models to show my one-of-a-kind pieces, and that will include participation in fashion trade shows, PR events, and many more modeling and traveling opportunities."

Even more women squealed and a few appeared to be praying for the opportunity to be chosen.

"You will each be judged in four categories by the panel you see before me." Taheim pointed to the team he and Winter had put together. "You were each told to bring tasteful lingerie and nightwear. We hate to sound harsh, but if you didn't come prepared or don't think you can give us the look we need, this fashion show isn't for you."

He wasn't surprised when three people got up and left.

"We understand how nerve-racking this can be," Winter started. "But if you want to make it in this industry, these are typical expectations. Keep in mind that we are judging you on your walk, personality, style and overall look."

"And please don't forget to place the number we assigned you on the top of your résumé. I hope each of you brought ten copies, as specified," Taheim added.

Taheim and Winter split the models into six groups

of seven, and then they took their seats at the table placed near the temporary runway that was set up for practice. Based on what he'd seen on Saturday and what he'd read on a few of the models' résumés, he was confident they had their top thirty or thirty-five models in the room.

Since they were the main designers and people planning the fashion show, it seemed natural that he and Winter sit next to each other. When the first two groups took the stage, he did a great job of concentrating. But when the lead Elite Events planner for the masquerade gala, Cydney Rayne-Miles—who had informed them that she would be late for judging—finally arrived, everyone seated at the table had to scoot closer to one another to make room.

Moving closer to Winter shouldn't have been a problem for him—except it meant that occasionally they would bump elbows.

"I didn't know you were left-handed," he said, noticing it for the first time.

"Yeah, sorry. I know we keep bumping into each other. Hope it's not too difficult for you to take notes."

Is she serious? Of course he was having trouble taking notes, but it wasn't because she was left-handed and kept brushing elbows with him. Her thigh was also leaning against his, and every time she tilted her head to the side to observe a model, her arousing scent—which smelled like a combination of lavender, vanilla and honey—made him want to close his eyes and get lost in her aroma.

"No, you're not making it too difficult," he lied. It wasn't that he wanted to lie. But saying *As a matter of fact, being this close to you makes me want to drag you to the nearest bed and dive into your sweetness with my tongue* wasn't exactly appropriate.

"You look stressed about something," she whispered close to his ear.

"I'm good." His voice sounded strained even to his own ears. When she leaned back, he could feel her eyes on him, and slowly, he felt the mood change.

He looked at her and noticed a sneaky smile on her face. Before he had a chance to ask her what she was up to, she placed her hand on his thigh.

He shot upright in his chair, barely stopping himself from standing up completely. Her laugh lightened the sexual tension.

"You find this funny?" he whispered back to her, keeping his eyes on the runway this time.

"A little," she said with a laugh. "Only because I could tell you were lying to me. I'll scoot over a little to give you more room."

As her hands went underneath her chair to scoot it over, his hand flew to her wrist.

"Don't move," he whispered.

Her eyes trailed from his hand on her wrist to his face. When she met his eyes, all laughter was gone from her gaze. They didn't say anything for a few seconds. He was too intrigued by her expression to say anything further. His eyes dropped down to her lips despite the fact that his mind warned him not to look. She'd covered them with a red tinted gloss. The shiny layer catching in the light was enough to make him think of several naughty ways he'd love to wipe all the shine off.

She must have sensed the direction of his thoughts,

because her lips slightly parted and a breath so faint he would have missed it had he not been so close escaped.

"If you two are done with whatever you're doing, group four is coming onstage soon," Autumn whispered as she leaned over Winter. "If you missed the last couple models, I'm sure you can look at the panel's notes, but I liked them."

Taheim looked on either side of him at the curious glances coming from the team, not surprised to see he'd even gotten the attention of Cydney, who had quirked her eyebrow as if to say *I told you so.*

When he felt someone's eyes on his back, he turned to find his brother standing near the main bar with a knowing gaze on his face.

He'd been pretty vocal when he'd discussed the fact that he would never be interested in Winter after they were set up on that blind date. But now that a few of their mutual friends were seeing them blatantly flirt with one another, it felt as if the joke was on them.

You will not flirt with Taheim. You will not flirt with Taheim. Winter chanted the words over and over again in her head as she made her way to his condo.

Even though she'd been there before for the bachelorette party that his sister had thrown, it felt different knowing that he was on the other side of the door waiting for her arrival. Back then he was just a guy she despised. *Now* he seemed to be the only man on her mind.

It should help that she wasn't visiting him for a date or anything too personal. She was there to get down to business. Today was her first day waiting on him hand and foot, since she'd lost the social media bet.

She hated to lose and from the social media results that she calculated, she'd only lost by a small percentage. She never backed down from a bet. Even though she had the feeling that Taheim would be holding this one over her head.

As she made her way up the stairs, she tried her best to slow her heart rate. "You can do this," she said to herself as she lifted her hand to hit the buzzer for the back door of his condo, as he'd told her to do the day before.

"Hello, it's Winter," she said into the speaker. Within seconds, the door buzzed and she made her way up the narrow stairway and was surprised to find him standing by the elevator.

"The back entrance is closer to my condo, but I figured since there aren't many people who take this way unless we live here, I'd meet you halfway."

"Thanks." She stood by him in silence when they stepped in the elevator car. It was Tuesday night and although they had just seen each other for the final auditions last week, she felt like a nervous teenager visiting a boy's house for the first time.

"I'm glad we found thirty-five models eager to be in the fashion show," he said, breaking the silence.

"Me, too." She ran her fingers through her curls as she watched the numbers slowly rise with each floor they passed. "I'm glad we chose some models with experience and some fresh faces, too. I think this is a great opportunity for them and I'm really eager to see who would be good for future Bare Sophistication projects."

"Same here. It was nice to have so many people excited about my city tour for Collegiate Life and T.R. Night."

"What you've accomplished is impressive. There were a lot of young men at the model call who really look up to you."

"Yeah, I like working with the younger generation. I remember some of them from when they were kids and used to come into one of my parents' first restaurants on the South Side of Chicago."

"That's right," Winter said, snapping her fingers. "Your parents own a chain of soul food restaurants in the Midwest, right?"

"They sure do," he said as they stepped off the elevator onto the twenty-fifth floor. "One of their newest restaurants isn't a soul food restaurant, though. Remember the place we had our first date?"

As if she'd forget. "Of course. I remember. They own that restaurant?"

"The previous owner was a friend of my dad's who passed away. He also told my dad if something happened to him, he wanted him to take over, so he did. Now it's one of three steak houses that my parents own. The one here in Chicago, one in Indianapolis, and another in Saint Louis."

"That's awesome."

He opened his door and motioned for her to step into his condo first. "I meant to tell you that your condo is gorgeous. Very tastefully decorated and spacious. I haven't seen anything like it since I've been in Chicago."

"Thanks, but you can thank my sister, Kaya, for putting her interior decorating degree to good use. And the reason it seems like one of a kind is because it is."

"There's that cockiness you hide so well."

"I'm serious," he said, motioning for her to follow him down the hallway. When they reached a set of sliding doors, just like the closets in his bedroom, they opened on their own.

"You must really like motion sensors, huh," she said with a laugh.

He looked over his shoulder and gave her a smirk. "Why open doors when you can place motion sensors in the floor?"

"Of course—why not?" she said as she threw her hands in the air. They were both still laughing as he took out a book and opened it to a picture collage.

"What is this?" she asked.

"It's a collage of how this building was originally going to look. The owners wanted to build a condo similar to those that they'd built in Miami, Atlanta and Phoenix. But when they bought this property, they realized that Chicago was unlike the other territories. Our weather is unpredictable and our city isn't like the others they'd built in. So when they came to R&W Advertising to create a marketing campaign for the property, my partners and I couldn't let them go through with it without offering some advice."

"How did they take your advice?"

"Bad at first," he said with a laugh. "But you know Daman Barker right?"

"Yeah, he's married to Imani with Elite Events and he's one of your partners at R&W Advertising, right?"

"Yes, he is. He also owns his father's company, Barker Architecture. I had set up a meeting with the owners of this building and Daman and his staff, and that's where the concept of this building was created."

He flipped through a few pages in the book. "Each condo is different and for the condos that were sold at the start of this project, we were able to pay extra to create them to our liking."

Winter glanced at the pictures taken during the development of the condo and was impressed by everything she saw. "Let me guess," she said as she glanced up at him. "You were the first person to purchase one of the condos?"

"Second, actually," he said with a laugh. "We're on the east wing and there is no penthouse on this side, so I'm the top condo. But Jaleen Walker, my other partner at R&W Advertising, beat me to the penthouse in the west wing on the twenty-sixth floor."

She laughed as she glanced around his office and looked down the hall. His condo was even more beautiful than she'd remembered. Especially since she hadn't really gotten a chance to admire everything in detail, since she'd been working.

I wonder how many women he's had here. She shook her head at the thought. It wasn't as if they were dating or anything. She was there to allow him to collect on the bet they'd made, not to fantasize about having sex with him on top of his massive desk.

"So," she said, clasping her hands together and standing up from the chair she had been sitting in. "What's on this list of things to do?"

He closed the book they'd been looking at and placed it back on his bookshelf. "You hate that you lost, don't you?"

"Well, you cheated," she said, crossing her arms over her chest. "You made it seem like there was more to our relationship than just business, so of course people started commenting on all our social media sites about it…including our friends."

He walked around his desk to stand in front of her. "Was I wrong in my assumption?" he asked in a husky voice. She took a step back. Studying her eyes, he took another step forward. "Isn't this more than just business?"

It wasn't so much what he was asking but rather the way in which he was asking that made her want to turn on her heels and run out the door. She was glad she hadn't removed her coat, because there was no doubt in her mind that her nipples had hardened and were probably peeking through her burgundy dress.

Standing there in his gray sweater and jeans, he looked casual and comfortable, whereas she felt like the complete opposite. She felt unraveled and awkward. Exposed, even.

That's what it is, she thought as he continued to look at her intensely. Taheim barely knew her, and quite frankly, she didn't know too much about him either. Since the first day they had met, they'd passed judgment on one another. Yet the more they got to know each other, the more Winter understood why people thought they'd be a good match.

But she didn't do serious relationships, and especially not with playboys like Taheim. She wasn't too keen on sharing, and from what she'd gathered from the female population since she'd moved to Chicago, Taheim was always in some type of spotlight. He was a ladies' man, the ultimate charmer. Everything about him oozed trouble for all women alike. A woman who kept a spotless house but a design studio that might seem disorganized and messy to some. A woman who enjoyed watching classic black-and-white movies, and a woman who'd rather go to an opera or art museum than a club or a bar. She wasn't his type *at all*, and the sooner she got that through her head, the better.

"So, what's first on your list of things you want me to do today?" she asked again, hoping he would pick up on her body language and stop the flirting.

"I've really been struggling with organizing my design studio, so I was hoping you could help me with that today."

Of course it's the one thing I can't seem to keep organized myself, she thought. "Of course," she said instead. "I can definitely help with that."

She turned and walked into the hallway, eager to escape the confines of his office. "Can I hang my coat in that closet over there?" She pointed to the same closet she had been hiding in when she'd gotten the call telling her that her top model wouldn't be able to make the bachelorette party.

"Sure," he said as he came up from behind her. When they reached the closet, she removed her coat and handed it to him, making sure she avoided eye contact. She didn't need to look him in the eye. She could feel his eyes roaming up and down her body, taking in her outfit.

"Did you design that dress yourself?"

Just last week, hoping that you would see me in it. "Yes, I did. It's the first time I'm wearing it." Her burgundy knit dress hit right above the knee and she'd paired it with some brown heel boots that covered her calves to keep her warm. Her hair was pulled back from her face with only a few tendrils framing her face.

"It's beautiful…"

She turned at the sound of his voice, noticing for the first time how close they were standing.

"Thank you."

He tilted his head to the side. "Are we going to go the entire day pretending that we're not attracted to each other?"

She sucked in a breath and willed her eyes to stay on his and not drop to his lips. "It's been working out for us so far."

"Not for me." His voice was strong. Definite. "You haven't been in my condo since I found you in my bedroom."

"Is that a problem?" Her tongue dipped out her mouth to lick her lips.

"The fact that I can't help but picture how you looked that night is definitely a problem."

She bit her lips.

"Don't do that," he said, stepping an inch or so closer to her.

"Do what?"

His gaze went from her lips to her eyes before landing on her lips again. "Bite your bottom lip. You can't do that."

She squinted her eyes as she observed his behavior. "Why can't I do that?" She was playing with fire, but at the moment, she really didn't care.

His eyes went back to hers. "You bite your lip when you are contemplating an idea. You also bite your lip when you're nervous about something. But you lick your lips when you're aroused."

She couldn't stop her eyes from growing big in surprise. She hadn't even been aware that she did that. Shifting from one leg to the other, she tried to squeeze her thighs together to stop the throbbing need she was faced with whenever she was around Taheim.

"You're aroused and nervous, aren't you? That's why you bit and licked your lips."

"Not really." She shrugged, trying to brush off his words. "What do I have to be nervous about?"

"What about the aroused part?"

Instead of responding, she just shrugged again.

"Exactly what I wanted to hear," he said as he snaked an arm around her waist.

She was going to inform him that she hadn't said anything, but his gaze penetrated right through her, locking the words in her mouth. All that she could focus on was the fact that his mouth was moving closer to hers.

You should stop this kiss before it happens. There were a hundred reasons floating around in her mind that warned her to step out of his embrace and tell him that their relationship would continue to be strictly professional. But the minute she felt his breath fan her lips, her arms curved around his neck and lightly cupped the back of his head.

"I've been waiting to do this since we met," he said right before his lips crashed into hers.

Chapter 7

Alarms went off in every section of his mind cautioning him not to deepen the kiss, but he refused to listen. In fact, he was certain nothing could pull him away from kissing her right now, even though he knew they had just blurred the professional line.

Winter tasted so delicious and the same smell he'd tried to ignore at the model call was back with a vengeance, demanding that he fill himself with the sweet taste of her lips.

Slowly, provocatively, he slipped his tongue between the edges of her mouth and relished in her sugary flavor. A thin layer of berry flavor mingled with her taste. Usually, Taheim wasn't into tasting any type of lip gloss when he was kissing a woman, because women in his past had always used too much, assuming it would make their lips more alluring. But not Winter. Her lips were soft. Inviting.

She stood on tiptoe and the curves of her body melted into his. His arms, which had been leisurely draped on the side of her waist, gripped her even tighter before moving slightly higher on the arch of her back.

When she moaned, he groaned in satisfaction, unable to remember the last kiss he'd had that felt this good…this *right*. He was convinced that one kiss from Winter would never satisfy his urge. But at least it would satisfy his curiosity so that he could focus on working with her without wanting to kiss her senseless.

Exploring her mouth was everything he'd known it would be and he felt the passion in each suckle. If he wasn't careful, he'd be too far gone to stop the kiss.

With all the strength he could muster, he broke the kiss but continued to keep her steady in his arms. He explored her eyes, preparing himself for the look of guilt or regret that might cross her facial features. They might be attracted to one another, but he didn't forget how much they had disliked each other. Even if they no longer felt that way and had seemed to start building an actual friendship, sometimes it was hard to flip off the dislike switch.

His desire rose another notch when instead of regret, her eyes reflected potent lust. Just like that, the bulge in his pants was starting to grow and take on a form that would be impossible to get down if he didn't step away from her.

"Maybe we really should get started on that list?" he suggested. The gentlemanly thing to do would be to apologize for kissing her. But he refused to say something he didn't mean and an apology would have been a lie.

"Yeah, let's get started on organizing your design studio. Where is it?"

·"It's right past the kitchen. I keep the door locked."

She smiled before she turned her back to him and began walking in the direction that he had pointed to.

"You won't start acting all weird on me now that we kissed," she said as she looked over her shoulder and winked at him. He hadn't expected her to reference the kiss at all.

"I won't if you won't."

She stopped walking and turned completely around to face him. "I wanted you to kiss me, so maybe if you look at it as something that would have eventually happened anyway, you won't be giving me that look as if you aren't sure what to say or how to act."

He blinked several times, wondering if he was imagining her saying those words or if she'd really said them. But from the sly look on her face, he knew she'd actually said them.

"Just being honest," she said with a shrug as she enclosed her arm around his. "Come on—time to organize."

After two hours of shuffling through fabric, buttons, various pieces of sewing equipment and sketches, they had his design studio more organized than it had been in ages. As much as he hated to admit it, having Winter there with him in his studio felt right. She didn't feel like someone he had really known only a few months.

Now he was on the sofa he kept in the studio for when he needed to take naps but didn't want to lose his muse. Winter was sitting adjacent to him on an artistic circular chair he'd won at an auction.

"So after getting a degree in business and advertising, you decided to go to the Art Institute of Chicago? Well, you're quite the entrepreneur."

"Sure did," he replied. "My parents thought I was crazy at first, but they knew I always liked to keep my hands on a few things. I took summer classes and finished business school in three years, then turned around and finished at the School of the Art Institute in three years, as well."

He leaned forward to the table stationed in front of him to take a swig from the beer bottle he'd grabbed when they'd finished organizing. "Did you always know you wanted to be a designer?"

Her smile was immediate. "I did. Actually, both my sisters and I always knew we wanted to be in the fashion industry. It probably has a lot to do with my dad. He was always flying us to different countries during any school break so that he could paint or sculpt masterpieces. It always seemed that every place we went, the clothing and garments were so different. We became obsessed with the many different styles in the countries we visited."

"That sounds like my type of childhood."

Her mouth was turned into a smile, but her eyes seemed sad when she spoke. "My dad is the best." Her eyes left his as he watched her get lost in thought. "My dad is from France, and before he became a painter and sculptor, he was an accountant at a major law firm in Paris. He met my mother while on a business trip in New York and she was working at a diner at the time. She was an aspiring actress and model, working to pay her way through acting school. They fell in love and my dad transferred to his firm's New York office. Within months, they moved to my mom's hometown in New Jersey and had my sisters and I. They're divorced now, though, and my dad is back living in France, following his dream."

When she grew quiet, he wanted to ask her more about her family, but he held back because he didn't want to dampen the mood. There was sadness in her voice that hadn't been there before. "So you went to the New York School of Design?"

"Yes, I did, and it was a life changer for me. During my schooling I met so many great designers, and after graduating, I spent two years visiting the top fashion countries as an apprentice for a major fashion designer. My dad even met me at a couple locations." Her voice perked up as she talked about her experience at design school.

"Similar to you, my sister Autumn went to the Parsons New School of Design and got a bachelor of business administration in design and management. She also participated in two programs that they offered that focused on helping students launch careers in the business side of the fashion industry. After she graduated, she decided to enroll in the Fashion Institute of Technology in New York."

"You and your sister really do love fashion," he said with a laugh.

"So does our younger sister, Summer. Always one to be different, Summer went to LA for her schooling and got a public relations degree with a concentration in fashion marketing. She's working between New York and Miami now for a top PR firm, but she is also a partner in Bare Sophistication. Autumn and I think she's trying to learn all she can before approaching us about opening boutiques in other locations."

"Your family is impressive," he said. "I love my brother and sister, but I'm not sure we could work that closely together. How far apart are you in age?"

"Summer is twenty-eight. Autumn just turned thirty, so we are the same age for a month each year. I'll be thirty-one the day after Christmas."

"I didn't know you were a Christmas baby." He gave her a quick glance over. "But I guess it seems fitting for a woman named Winter to have been born in winter."

"Ha, very funny. Whatever jokes you're cooking up, I've heard them all."

"Then I'll save my breath," he said with a laugh. "So you get your creativity from your dad. What do you get from your mom?"

What do you get from your mom? His question lingered in the air unanswered. It wasn't that she was ignoring him. His question was valid given how much she talked about her dad. But she really didn't know how to respond, since the minute she was old enough to understand the troubles in her parents' marriage, she'd told herself she was nothing like the woman who'd given birth to her. They might have looked the same, been the same height and had the same complexion, but that was where the comparisons stopped. At least, that was where Winter hoped they stopped.

She glanced at Taheim, knowing that it wasn't fair to remain silent. "Nothing," she finally said.

The look on his face proved that he wanted to know

more. She hoped her facial expression showed that she didn't want to talk about the subject any further. Talking about her mom always put her in a bad mood. When she visited her mom's older sister, Cynthia Madden, in Arkansas, she'd often wonder why in the world she'd gotten stuck with Sonia Dupree, when her male cousins had the best mom in the world.

"So I'm curious," he said, seemingly trying to break the awkwardness. "How do three sisters all with various fashion degrees decide to open a lingerie boutique and not a clothing boutique?"

"Good question," she said with a laugh that forced thoughts of her mother out of her mind. "Our dad wondered the same thing when we told him about our dream. But for us, there was never any other option. You know that feeling a man gets when he's tried on his first pair of name-brand gym shoes? You know, the kind represented by a top athlete that every kid in school wants their parents to buy them?"

"Of course I remember that. For me it was my first pair of black-and-red Air Jordan sneakers."

"Exactly. We wanted to make women feel that way. We wanted women to put on a piece of our lingerie and feel empowered and sexy at the same time. No matter your shape or size, loving yourself is difficult for some women. We were raised in a society that tries to tell us the right and wrong way to look. Your self-image is important and not all of us are a size-two tall-and-slender model type. We have curves. We have thighs. We have butts, breasts. We may be bony or we may be thick. But one thing we all have in common as women is the ability to love our body image and ourselves just as we are, even if the world disagrees."

She watched his mouth slowly curve into a smile. "I think that message is a great one and extremely necessary for today's generation."

She gave him a playful look. "So now you agree with what I said at that fund-raising dinner we attended last month? Young women need good role models just as much as men."

"I never disagreed."

She turned up one eyebrow. "Let's not get into that again."

"Deal." He got up and grabbed a pamphlet from a built-in drawer on the wall opposite where they were sitting.

"Whenever I speak to youth groups about following your dreams, this is the pamphlet I pass out to them." He handed it to her. She skimmed the first few pages, paying close attention to the mission statement.

She read aloud the last words in the statement. "'Nurture your idea. Cultivate your goals. Chase the dream.'"

She glanced up at him. "I love the mission of Collegiate Life."

"Thanks," he said, reclaiming a seat on the sofa. "A percentage of all my sales goes to a charity here in Chicago that helps young men get off the streets. The charity also allows them to take classes to help prepare them for the workforce as long as they have their GED or are aspiring to get it."

"I'm impressed," she replied as she nodded her head.

"Impressed that the Collegiate Life brand isn't just your average clothing line or impressed that you and I have more in common than you thought?"

"A little bit of both." Placing the pamphlet on the

table, she picked up the glass of wine that Taheim had poured her when they had finished organizing the studio.

As she took a sip, her eyes caught his over the rim of the glass, and she wasn't surprised to find him staring at her suggestively.

"What's on your mind?" she dared to ask.

"You inspire me," he said sincerely. "I haven't had that feeling in an extremely long time."

She took another quick sip of her wine and tried to laugh it off. "I'm sure you say that to all the women who enter your studio." She batted her eyes to emphasize the humor in her statement. She couldn't look at him yet. If she did, he'd probably be able to sense that she was fishing for the number of women he'd brought into his condo. *Why do I even care?* She shouldn't be concerned about what he did.

"The women I date don't inspire me." Her eyes flew to his at his statement. "In fact, I have a section down the hall for entertaining company. I don't invite women to my bedroom and I definitely don't invite them into my studio."

I'm the first woman who's been in his studio? Interesting. "Well, you didn't exactly invite me into your bedroom," she said with a smile. "Your sister did."

After a few seconds of silence, he leaned his elbows on his knees and clasped his hands together. "I have a proposition for you."

Oh man, please don't proposition me, because it will be extremely difficult to say no. "What is it?"

"Lately, I haven't been inspired by much of anything, and although at first I thought I was maybe just overworked or tired, I see now that's not the case. For the rest of the week, since you lost the bet, I want you to help me find my muse."

Her forehead creased in confusion. "And how, pray tell, do you propose I do that?" Winter always told people that she was up for doing anything at least once…if she was given full disclosure of what that something was.

"By helping me get inspired to finish the T.R. Night collection."

"You're struggling with T.R. Night?"

"Yes, and you just so happen to specialize in lingerie and nightwear."

"For women, yes, but I don't create a lot of male pieces."

"But you can, right?" he asked, hopeful. "Or at least give me suggestions?"

It broke her heart to hear the desperation in his voice. Searching his eyes, she realized there was a possibility he was suffering through what most designers feared…the day you lost your creativity.

"I'll help you," she said, knowing she couldn't leave him hanging. "Except I leave town on Friday and will be gone for a week. I had actually planned on telling you as soon as I got to your condo, but it slipped my mind." She didn't add the fact that his entire presence sometimes made her lose her focus. "My staff is well aware of where we stand with the plans for the fashion show, and if I have time between states, I'll fly back here to check on things."

"Between states? Where are you going?"

"First I'm headed to Las Vegas for an international fashion trade show and a really artsy lingerie theater performance. Then I'm headed to Kauai, Hawaii, to assist with the styling of a swimsuit photo shoot. I have friends in both places and was invited months before I knew we had to do the Inferno fashion show here in Chicago."

"That's perfect," Taheim said as he stood and began pacing the room.

"What's perfect?" She stood up when he didn't respond right away. She could barely hear what he was mumbling since he seemed to be talking more to himself than her. "What's perfect, Taheim?" she asked again.

He stopped pacing to look directly at her. "You said you would help me, right?"

"I did," she said hesitantly.

"Then that's perfect." He placed a hand on each of her shoulders. "I'm long overdue for a vacation, and you're right—our teams are capable of handling the planning while we're gone. There won't be any T.R. Night collection to show if I can't get inspired to create more pieces. So if you're okay with it, I'd like to accompany you on your trip."

Her mouth dropped before she could catch it. She searched his eyes for any sign of humor.

"But I leave in three days."

"I only need a few hours to pack."

"Oh my goodness, you're serious?"

His lips curled to the side. "Dead serious."

Chapter 8

"She really said it was okay for you to go with her to Vegas and Hawaii?"

"Of course she did. Why do you seem so shocked?" Taheim asked, keeping his voice low.

Ajay gave him a look of disbelief. "Oh, I don't know, could it be the fact that up until a few weeks ago, you two still couldn't stand each other? Or maybe it's the fact that you once described her as the worst date you'd ever had. And my favorite reason as to why this is a bad idea, how about the fact that both of you are planning the fashion show for Inferno's grand opening? When you get back, you will only have a couple weeks left to plan."

Taheim looked around Inferno to see if anyone was within earshot. It was the final practice before he and Winter were going out of town tomorrow. Even though the planning would continue in their absence, they wouldn't be available in person to iron out all the details if something went wrong or needed to be changed.

He placed a reassuring hand on his brother's shoulder. "Don't worry, Ajay—we got this. And you know I was worried about creating some of the final wow pieces for T.R. Night, so I really think this trip will help me."

"If you say so," he said just before Autumn reached them.

"Hey, guys," she said, looking from one to the other as if she'd overheard part of the conversation. "Ajay, I was wondering if you could ensure that we order some gluten-free options next time we have a practice."

"Do any of the models only eat gluten-free?" Ajay asked. "Because I can order them something gluten-free."

"I'm the one who's inquiring. You should always offer other options and healthy options."

His eyebrows scrunched together. "I have vegetables and fruit on that snack table, so I thought I was being healthy."

"But there's also quesadillas, tacos, tortilla chips..."

"And I have guacamole, peppers and low-fat cheese," he interjected.

Autumn's lips grew tight in frustration. "Listen, it was just a suggestion. Buy whatever you want."

Taheim didn't laugh until she walked away. "What in the world was that about?"

"Man, I don't know. I swear Autumn has an opinion about everything."

"Really," Taheim said, looking at her and Winter

interact with the models. "She seems so cool when I talk to her."

Ajay huffed. "She is, until she's rattling off statistics and telling me what to do. Can you believe the other day she asked me about the tattoo on my arm? The one of the cross with the word *hope* written inside it."

"What's so bad about asking about your tattoo?"

"Nothing, except she asked me why I got it and I told her that it symbolized a rough time in my life when I was frustrated with how things were turning out."

Taheim nodded as he thought back to the time when things hadn't been so good for Ajay. "I'm guessing you didn't like her response."

"You know me, bro. I'm not the type to open up, and even though I didn't tell her much, I said enough. Afterward, she looked at me and asked if I realized that a tattoo was just inserting ink into the dermis layer of the skin and that a study showed that one-third of people who got tattoos regretted it."

Taheim laughed again. "It's not like she said anything bad."

"That was just the beginning. She has a stat or opinion about everything. I remember just staring at her, thinking that I now realize how you must have felt when Winter went off on you during your blind date."

As if they knew they must be talking about them, both Winter and Autumn turned to face Taheim and Ajay.

"Those Dupree sisters are something else," Ajay said, shaking his head and taking a sip of his drink.

"They sure are," he agreed. Taheim heard his brother

continue to talk, but he wasn't really listening to what he was saying, since he was too busy locking eyes with Winter.

"Can you stop staring at him long enough for us to wrap up this practice?" Autumn asked. "When you agreed to do this fashion show, I didn't know that meant I'd have to work with Mr. Grumpy."

Winter broke eye contact with Taheim to glance at her sister. "Ajay is one of the most down-to-earth men that I've met here in Chicago. Are you sure it's him and not you?"

"I'm sorry, but did you just say what I think you said?"

"Autumn, I love you like crazy but you are a little difficult to deal with sometimes, only to the people who don't know you."

"Whether people know or understand me, rude is rude no matter how you slice it."

"And sometimes the things you say sound judgmental," Winter replied. "I'm not saying Ajay wasn't rude to you. But I am saying that maybe you need to think about what you say before you say it."

"Whatever. Enough about me. Why on earth did you tell Taheim he could accompany you on your trip?"

"I already told you why. He said he needed some inspiration and he's right. What better way to be inspired for a clothing line than to attend a few out-of-state fashion events."

Winter twirled her finger at Danni so that she would tell the models to walk down the runway again.

"Are you sure that's all it is?"

She looked from the models to Autumn. "What other reason would I have?" Even as she said the words aloud, she knew Autumn would pick up on the words left unsaid.

He might have invited himself on the trip, but she had to admit, she was looking forward to having him come along.

Despite their obvious differences, they shared a lot of similarities, and when they had been in his studio, she'd realized that she also enjoyed talking to him. After she'd agreed to let him accompany her on the trip, they'd talked for another hour. What she'd enjoyed even more about the rest of their talk was that it was casual, friendly, even. After the fiery kiss they'd shared, it had been easier to naturally flirt with each other.

"Earth to Winter," Autumn said, breaking into her thoughts. "Do you even want to know how many seconds you spent clearly focused on him and not the models who did a second run-through because you requested it?"

Her cheeks grew warm with embarrassment. "That's all for today, folks. Autumn and Danni will have another practice with you next week and then Taheim and I will meet with you all when we get back in town."

Out of the corner of her eye, she caught Autumn and Danni share a knowing look. She was just about to say something sarcastic to them when a few voices behind her got her attention.

When she turned, Taheim was making his way to her.

"Hey, do you have a second to meet my mom?" he asked, motioning toward the bar, where Ajay stood with their sister, Kaya, and the woman she assumed to be Taheim's mother. "She wants to meet the Bare Sophistication team."

Winter opened her mouth to say something, but no words came out. Meet his mother? Hadn't he gotten the memo? Winter Dupree *did not* meet parents of the opposite sex. She'd learned in high school that it didn't matter if she was just friends with the guy, dating the guy or just doing a school project with a guy—parents always loved her and alluded to a more serious relationship.

In this case, Taheim was just starting to become a friend… A friend she was attracted to… A friend she was attracted to who no doubt had a reputation. She didn't want to meet his mother. She couldn't meet his mother.

"Danni and I would love to meet her, too," Autumn chimed in, motioning for Danni to come down from the stage.

"Great, follow me."

As soon as he turned his back to them, Winter shot Autumn a look of irritation. "What the heck are you doing? I don't do parents."

"Suck it up. I just saved you from looking like an idiot. You were just standing there not saying anything."

"That's because I was trying to see how I could tell him no without it sounding like a brush-off."

"News flash. His mom was looking at you the entire time Taheim was talking to you. There was no way you were going to be able to get out of this."

Since all eyes were still on her, she didn't respond

and instead continued to follow Taheim on what felt like the longest walk across a wood floor *ever*.

"Mom, this is Winter Dupree, Autumn Dupree and Danni Allison."

"Ladies, this is my mom, Regina Reed."

"It's very nice to meet you," his mom said as she shook each of their hands. Winter looked from Kaya to her mom, thinking the two looked a great deal alike. *Kinda the way my mom and I favor each other.* She shivered at the unwelcome reminder of her mother.

"It's nice to meet you, Mrs. Reed."

Regina looked at all three women before setting her gaze on Winter. "So you're the woman who has my son's nose wide open."

"Ma," Taheim said quickly.

"Oh, hush, son. I only meant that I admire a woman who would go on a terrible blind date with you and then turn around and let you accompany her on a trip. You're pretty lucky, if you ask me." She gave Winter a once-over. "She's beautiful, and from what I hear from your brother about that date, she's got a smart mouth to keep you in check, too."

Oh, I like her, Winter thought as she shared a look of surprise with Autumn. "Mrs. Reed, your son and I aren't dating."

"I never said you were," she replied with a laugh. "Although I would love for him to stop dating random women and settle down and have some babies, I want him to make sure it's with the right woman."

Was that a dig at me? She wasn't sure, but she definitely felt as though all the attention was on her.

"Winter, why don't you join me in that booth over there so we can have a chat?"

She followed the direction of Regina's finger and tried her best to stop her heart from beating out of her chest. *Have a chat? About what?*

Regina started walking toward the booth. "That wasn't a question, dear. Follow me."

After a quick nudge from Autumn, Winter fell in line behind Mrs. Reed before taking a seat across from her in the booth.

"So you're the creative vision behind Bare Sophistication?"

"Yes, I've designed every piece in our store."

"That's impressive. I can tell you're very driven. Both my sons and my daughter think very highly of you."

"You have raised wonderful children."

"Thank you. And what about your parents? Are you close to them?"

"My parents are divorced, but I'm extremely close to my dad. I definitely get my creativity and drive from him. He realized his dreams a little later in life, but once he did, he went after them and succeeded. I'm so proud of him."

"I'm sure he's proud of you, too." Her eyes grew more inquisitive. "What about your mother? Are you both close?"

I was hoping you wouldn't ask that. "Actually, we aren't," Winter said honestly. "We look alike, but our similarities stop there."

"Why aren't you close?"

Winter sighed as she tried to think about the best way to explain her mother. "Mrs. Reed, you know how some women, like yourself, just have that natural motherly quality about them? Whether you've always had it or developed it when you had kids? Though all mothers don't mother their children the same, in their own unique way, their children know they care about them."

"Of course, sweetie. I understand exactly what you mean. I live and breathe for my children."

"Well, my mother isn't like that. She didn't get bit by the motherly bug." *Hell, the good-wife bug didn't bite her either.* For the first time in a while, Winter wanted to actually explain her frustration with her mother with no filter. Maybe it was the sincerity in Regina's eyes or the fact that her bluntness made her easier for Winter to talk to.

"Winter, do you know why I wanted to speak to you privately?"

She shook her head before answering. "No, ma'am."

"I wanted to talk to you because I know my son, and from what I hear from my other children and what I saw in him today, he's becoming quite fond of you."

Winter was hesitant at first but then decided to continue. "I'm becoming quite fond of your son, as well."

"I can see that," she said, giving Winter a smile. "But as much as he tries to act tough, his heart is delicate. Be careful with it and give him time to open up. When he does, I guarantee that you'll see they don't come any better than my son."

Spoken like a true mom. They weren't even dating and already his mom was warning her not to hurt her son. She liked her. She liked her a lot.

"I understand, Mrs. Reed."

"I can tell you do. I see it in your eyes."

As Mrs. Reed made her way out the booth, Winter

had to refrain from asking her what other things she saw in her eyes.

"Oh, and, Winter," she said as if remembering a part she'd forgotten to say, "some women are weak-minded and others have a strong sense of self. Just because your mother seems to only think about her-self, doesn't mean she doesn't love you. Sometimes we don't know how to show love the right way, because we were never taught how to love ourselves in the first place. Have you told your mom how you feel?"

"I have, years ago. But I haven't seen my mom in over three years."

"Then the next time you see her, tell her how you feel. I don't know what you have gone through with your mom, but I do know that the hurt I felt from you today isn't fair to you or her. You deserve to tell her how you feel." She gave Winter a gentle hug and left her to contemplate the words she'd just said.

Chapter 9

"I don't know about you, but seventy-degree weather beats fifteen-degree weather any day," Taheim said as he stepped outside of the airport terminal.

Winter laughed as she handed her luggage to the taxi driver. "I agree! I love living in Chicago, but I always figured when I moved away from the East Coast, I would move someplace warmer. *Not* someplace equally as cold."

When their luggage was loaded, Winter gave the driver the address to the hotel they were staying at in Vegas.

"How many times have you been here?"

"Hmm, probably about five. What about you?"

"I think it's my fifth time, too, but Vegas never gets old."

They drove in comfortable silence for the first five minutes of the drive until they got closer to the Strip.

Taheim tore his gaze from the mountains in the distance to glance at Winter. "I'm not sure what you said to my mom, but she really likes you." He would have gone to the booth after his mom left yesterday and checked on Winter, but she'd left with her sister shortly after.

"I really enjoyed talking to your mom. She's blatantly honest, but the best part of our talk was hearing the love in her voice when referring to you and your siblings."

"Yeah, she's one of those moms who loves to brag on her kids." After his mom had spoken with Winter, she'd told him not to mess up the possibility of a relationship with her.

"She seems great, although I meant to ask…where was your dad?"

"Right now he's in Saint Louis overseeing the opening of a new restaurant."

"Wow, your parents are movers and shakers."

"Much like their children," he said with a wide smile.

Their conversation was stalled when they arrived at their massive casino hotel smack-dab in the middle of the Strip. As they walked to the check-in concierge, Taheim couldn't help but entertain the idea of them sharing the same room. Ten minutes later, he wondered if while he was doing all that thinking, Winter had slipped the woman who had checked them in an extra twenty bucks to guarantee they would be as far away from each other as possible.

"Okay, so the lingerie theater performance is in three hours. How about we meet down here in two hours and take a taxi together. It's taking place at a hotel at the beginning of the Strip." She stepped on an elevator opposite the one he'd be taking since their rooms were on separate wings of the hotel.

"Sounds like a plan. I'll meet you in the lobby." As Taheim made his way to his room, he thought about the fact that this was the first time he'd been to Vegas with a woman. The other four times had always been with a group of male friends for a bachelor party or birthday, with the exception of the last time he was there—to celebrate a friend's divorce from his cheating wife.

He entered his room and immediately dropped his luggage and walked over to the window to check out the view. There were many reasons why he loved Vegas, but he had to admit that the view was definitely high on his list.

They were going to be in Vegas for only a couple days, but he definitely wanted to make the most of it.

Taheim glanced at his black watch with blue-and-silver trimmings, satisfied that he had made it to the lobby five minutes early. He knew it wouldn't make up for the being extremely late the first time they went out, but he hoped she noticed his punctuality.

Unsure of how to dress for the night, he'd settled on dark jeans and a white button-up that he paired with an indigo blazer and black loafers. His entire outfit was from his Collegiate Life clothing line, which begged him to ask the question, *I wonder if Winter will be wearing some of her own lingerie pieces underneath her outfit.* In fact, he was pretty sure that she probably wore only pieces that she made. "Thinking about what she wears under her clothes is going to make the night drag," he whispered to himself.

There were plenty of ladies out today and he was getting more than enough attention. But his mind wasn't on any of those women. Mainly because ever since he'd caught Winter in his bedroom, his mind hadn't had much room to think about anyone else.

He whipped his head to the side of the lobby at the sound of a person jumping up and down near a slot machine.

Hmm, maybe I need to get in a little time at the slots. Tonight was the performance and tomorrow they would be at the trade show all day, so the trip didn't really allow much time for gambling.

Mind made up, he began walking toward the slot machines when he heard Winter calling his name. He took a couple more steps before he turned around to the direction of her voice, ready to tell her that he'd actually arrived early. But the minute he turned around, any thought he had was gone.

"Shit!" *How in the world am I supposed to focus with her wearing that?* Winter walked with grace and style across the lobby to meet him. The gentlemanly thing to do would be to meet her halfway. Unfortunately, there was nothing gentlemanly about him right now. Not his demeanor, not his body's reaction and definitely not his thoughts.

When she got closer to him, his mouth watered at how the strapless mint-green lace dress hugged her every curve like body paint. He assumed the white garment draped across her arm was a jacket, but his eyes didn't linger long enough to truly notice. He was too busy making his way down her toned legs to her feet, covered in matching mint-green heels.

Her makeup was flawless as usual and her brown curls were pinned to one side of her head, showing off her long elegant neck. A neck he wanted to nip… and bite…and suckle. *Lord. Have. Mercy.* He wasn't going to be able to survive the night.

"Were you heading to the slot machines?" she asked when she reached him.

"Um, yeah, I was." *Keep it short and sweet*, he thought. *That way you won't have to formulate too many words.*

"Did you still want to play the slots? We have about fifteen or so minutes to spare."

"I'm good. Let's just head to the show."

She squinted her eyes, clearly picking up on his strange behavior. *She comes down here in a dress like that, yet she's looking at me like I'm the crazy one.* He was irritated. Sexually frustrated. Pissed that he couldn't touch her. Confused as to why he couldn't touch her. Mad that he couldn't claim her in front of all the other drooling men around them. Hell, you name it, he felt it.

After they'd gotten in the taxi, arrived at the show, claimed their prime-location seats and gotten backstage passes so that Winter could see her friends before the show, he still felt irritated.

"Nick. Brian. How are you guys?" Winter said excitedly as she made her way through all the people backstage and raced toward two men who were both shirtless.

"Damn, you look good, girl."

"You do, too, Nick," she said, returning his hug.

"Mmm, I guess Chicago is doing you good, huh?"

"It's great, Brian," she said, giving him an equally friendly hug.

Man, she's hugging them awfully tight. Taheim had never been the jealous type, but watching Winter fawn all over two shirtless men was enough to make him want to punch something. Especially since he was inwardly giving his soon-to-be blue balls a pep talk.

He grabbed a water bottle off a nearby tray and was glad to feel the liquid slide down his throat and cool him off a little.

"Nick, Brian, this is my friend Taheim Reed."

"Oh, wait, *the* Taheim Reed of Collegiate Life?" Brian asked.

Okay, maybe they're not so bad, Taheim thought. "Yes, that's me."

"It's nice to meet you, man," he said, shaking hands with Taheim. "I'm Winter's ex-boyfriend."

Nope, still don't like the dude. Taheim's ears perked up with awareness. "Ex-boyfriend?"

"Yes, we dated during the second half of her junior year of college."

"Oh, did you, now," Taheim said, glancing from Brian to Winter.

"Yup, but that was only after Nick here dated her the first half of her junior year in college."

What the hell? "Oh, so you both dated Winter in college."

"It's a funny story," Nick said.

I doubt it, he thought. "What is it?" he asked, instead.

"I think I may walk around a little to get a feel for

the show," Winter said, slowly backing away from the three men.

First she introduces me to two ex-boyfriends and then she leaves me to chat with them? There was one thing he knew for sure. He'd been experiencing numerous firsts since he'd met Winter.

"Well, Winter actually dumped me for Brian," Nick said as he gripped Brian's shoulder.

"Yup, but then she dumped me because she said I reminded her too much of Nick."

Scratch that—I did need to hear this story. "So she dumped you both during the same year?"

"Sure did. Ultimately, I think it was because she and I were getting too close," Nick said. "Winter's not exactly the best at commitment."

"Meaning she cheated on you?"

"Oh no, never that. That's one thing Winter Dupree is definitely not. She and I had a lot of fun together."

"Then what did she do?" Taheim asked as he took another swig of water.

"Let's just say we were better off as friends. I should have known that our relationship was platonic when we posed nude to paint each other, but didn't end up having sex afterward."

Taheim began coughing uncontrollably, cursing the fact that he'd chosen that moment to drink water. "Sorry, it went down the wrong pipe. You were saying?"

Brian and Nick looked at one another before looking back to Taheim.

"Listen, if you choose to date Winter, all you have to know is that she's extremely loving and extremely loyal and is definitely one of the most creative people I've ever met in my life," Nick said.

Taheim looked at both men. "Then why didn't either of you ever get back together with her after college?"

"Should we tell him?" Brian asked Nick.

"I think that's best," Nick replied.

Brian turned to Taheim. "Well, Nick and I met at a bar and began talking about how we had both been dumped. Nick months before, and me more recently. After comparing notes, we realized it was by the same woman."

"But we both learned something valuable that night," Nick added as he looked at Brian before looking back at Taheim. "Being with Winter helped us both open up in ways we'd never imagined. She just has that effect on people."

Nick nudged Brian in his side. "And probably the most valuable lesson we learned that night was that we were both more attracted to each other than Winter."

Taheim wasn't sure how his face looked, but a deer caught in headlights seemed like a pretty accurate guess. "Oh," he said, trying to find more words and coming up short.

"The three of us have been good friends ever since, and now Nick and I, who were always made for Broadway, have our own show right here in Vegas," Brian said as he glanced at his phone and read a text message. "And speaking of friends, we told Winter that we were down a man yesterday and she just texted me that you may want to be in our show if we can guarantee that we will have an entire show dedicated to nothing but the T.R. Night collection you're releasing early next year."

"We sell out our 8:00 p.m. and 10:00 p.m. shows every night and there are three hundred seats at this venue, so the exposure would be phenomenal."

Taheim glanced around backstage, barely able to process everything that was being thrown at him. "Where is Winter?"

Just as the question left his mouth, his phone dinged with a text from her. She let him know that she had gone back to their seats and told him that it would be great exposure for his new line if he agreed to be in tonight's show.

"What exactly would I have to do?"

"Not that much," Brian said excitedly. "You'll only be in one scene and you just have to follow the other animals walking around and do what they do onstage."

Follow the what? "Did you just say *animals*?"

"People in animal costumes," Nick clarified.

Taheim looked from one man to the other, thinking the entire night seemed like one really big joke. On one hand, the opportunity was an extremely great one. But on the other hand, he didn't really know the details of the show and he really couldn't jeopardize his image doing something too outside the box without thinking it through first.

"Will my face be covered?"

"Completely. You'd be wearing an animal-print mask."

"So no one will know it's me under there?"

"No one except for us and Winter. That's it. And we won't say a word about this. We can even draw up disclaimer forms before you go on if it would make you more comfortable."

I can't believe I'm actually contemplating this. The only other time he'd done something this crazy was when one of the guys he'd gone to college with had wanted everyone in his wedding party to dress up like zombies. It had been like playing a part in *The Walking Dead* throughout the entire wedding and reception.

"Okay, I'll do it. As long as my identity is concealed."

"Excellent!"

When Brian grabbed him by the shoulders, shuffled him into a dressing room and pulled out some tiny tiger-print briefs and a tiger mask, it took all his energy not to run in the opposite direction.

"Um, where is the rest of this costume?"

"Oh, it's right here," Brian said as he handed him some cuffs and other accessories with the same tiger print.

"No additional clothing?"

Brian gave him a confused look. "Winter told you this was a lingerie show, right?"

"Yeah, she did. I was just hoping for a little more… material to cover the goods."

"No can do. There is an audience full of men and women waiting to see your goods, so that's the last thing we want to cover," he said as he tilted his head to the side before his eyes roamed over Taheim.

"Almost forgot," Brian said right when he got to the door. "Don't forget to growl while you're onstage. There's no need to crawl like you'll see some of the others do, but you'll have to growl."

As soon as the door closed, Taheim dropped to the

nearby stool and ran his fingers down his face. "Shit just got real," he said to himself as he tried to figure out exactly how he'd gotten himself into this mess.

Chapter 10

"Oh, and the best part was definitely when you started clawing at the sky like all the other animals and let out that loud growl before you left the stage."

"Listen," Taheim said as they continued walking around the trade show. "Aren't you tired of talking about me prancing around onstage last night in that costume?"

Winter looked up to the ceiling and placed one finger on her chin as if she were really contemplating his question.

"Um, nope. I'm definitely not done talking about it." Teasing him was way too much fun. Especially since she'd never thought that he would actually go through with it.

She would also never let him know that the first thing she'd felt when he walked onstage hadn't been laughter at all.

"Even if you didn't enjoy your performance, Nick and Brian thought you did a great job."

He smiled at her. "Thanks. They're cool dudes. But I definitely didn't know we were going to a show that was being planned by your ex-boyfriends."

She gave him a shy smile. "Given the fact that they are obviously more attracted to each other than me, I didn't think it was necessary to tell you. Besides," she said as she playfully hit him on the arm, "I didn't know they were going to tell you that I'd dated both of them, and had you not been so busy trying to hide the fact that you were jealous, you would have noticed their interaction with each other."

She stopped walking when she noticed Taheim was no longer walking beside her. "Why did you stop walking?"

"Do you see this face?"

She laughed at the stern look on his face. "And your point is…"

"My point is, this conversation is done. I'm glad Nick and Brian will have an entire show dedicated to T.R. Night nightwear, but that was my first and last time ever participating in a theater show. What I participated in last night doesn't get back to Chicago, are we clear?"

"Yes, sir," she said, saluting him and holding back another laugh.

They had been at the fashion trade show for four hours, and although the event had offered some great networking opportunities, she wished she could take a nap before they reached their destination.

"So, we're going to a fashion show?"

"Yes, a friend of mine is performing for a world-renowned European designer. He used to be a rock singer, but now he's a music producer in London."

"Ah, so it's another *he*."

"Aww, is that a hint of jealousy I hear in your voice?"

"Not at all," he said, shaking his head with a laugh. "I just wasn't aware that I was accompanying you on a trip to visit all your exes."

She laughed along with him. "Well, I assure you that Rocco and I only went on a couple dates…nothing serious. And he's happily engaged now to a beautiful woman he's been with for four years."

"Are you talking about Rocco Channing?"

"Yes, but of course, when I knew him, he was performing in bars and cafés here in the States. Have you met him?"

"Actually, I have," Taheim said as Winter handed their tickets to the woman standing outside the door for the fashion show. "I attended a fashion event in London with a few classmates right after we graduated and he was seated at a bar in the host hotel right by us. The introductions were short, but he talked to our group for a few minutes before my friend Grant pulled him aside to talk his ear off about starting a future in music."

"That sounds like Rocco," she said with a laugh. "Always making new friends."

When they walked into the ballroom, it was just as beautiful as Winter had imagined it would be.

"Wow, this is pretty nice," Taheim said as he followed her to their seats. They made it just in time to see Rocco come onstage to kick off the fashion show. It was always great seeing people go after their dreams and succeed.

The fashion show was amazing and seeing the breathtaking European designs cross the runway inspired her for a new lingerie line that she couldn't wait to sketch when they got back to the hotel. Rocco's intermission and final performances were even better than the first one.

"Rocco asked that we wait here for him," Winter informed Taheim after she read the message he'd texted her.

"I haven't seen an editorial fashion show like that in a while. Most of the fashion shows I've been attending lately are street or urbanwear with the occasional business fashion intertwined." She watched him glance around the room, enjoying the look of awe in his eyes.

"Lately, it seems that the audience for the fashion shows I attend or participate in tends to include celebrities, movie stars, hip-hop artists and singers. I can't recall the last time there were more high-fashion designers in a room than celebrities."

"Sometimes it's good to change up the scene and get out of our comfort zone and allow our creative expression to grow and flourish."

"I agree. But every now and then, life just gets in the way." He draped his arm across the back of her chair and Winter shivered at the closeness. "Have you always attended fashion shows?"

She turned slightly to him and smiled. "Ever since I was a young girl, I've always loved going to fashion shows. There's something about the runways, photographers, industry professionals and of course the unique clothing styles and designs that has always made me feel at home."

Taheim nodded his head in agreement. "I know the feeling. For me it wasn't fashion shows that made me feel that way—it was music videos."

Winter leaned over to ask him for more details, only briefly closing her eyes to take a quick whiff of his appetizing scent.

"Besides the music, what did you love about music videos?"

"Well, I'm not sure if you'll agree, but today's music videos aren't anything like what they used to be."

"I agree completely," she said with a laugh.

"Growing up, I felt like artists not only cared about the message they were sending through music, but they also used their videos as a way to display the latest trends in clothes, shoes and hairstyles. It was a form of creative expression. A way for them to reach a wide audience of people and defy what was considered the norm in fashion. I'm not saying we don't have artists around that do that now, but back in the day, most of the videos released were trendsetters… the first of their kind. When I initially released Collegiate Life, I knew I wanted to target the eighteen-to-thirty age market with an emphasis on the college scene. But somehow the Collegiate Life brand grew to lengths that I never saw coming. Before I knew it, I was still keeping my urban-meets-business flare but also creating clothing for the thirty-plus market, as well…for those who probably remember music videos the way I do."

"I knew I liked you when I first met you," a voice said from behind Winter and Taheim.

"Hey, Rocco," Winter said, standing up to give him

a hug. She turned to face Taheim. "Rocco, this is my friend Taheim Reed."

"Yeah, I remember you from when we met in London some years ago," Rocco said as he leaned out to shake his hand. "I never did get a chance to ask who designed that jacket you were wearing."

"Actually that design is part of my Collegiate Life clothing line now. As soon as Winter mentioned that we were seeing you perform, I told her about that night, but I wasn't sure you would remember me since my friend Grant was talking to you nonstop about starting a career in music."

"Did he ever get that career started?"

"Nope," Taheim said with a laugh. "A few months after that trip, he began teaching at an art school in Chicago and married, and now he has a baby on the way. But every now and then, he talks about what could have been."

"Speaking of marriage, would you both like to have dinner with me and my fiancée? She was backstage for the first half of the show until she had to tend to some business, but Vanessa would love to see you again, Winter."

Winter glanced at Taheim, who nodded his head in agreement. "We'd love to."

As they followed Rocco out of the exhibit hall to his parked car, she wondered if Taheim was feeling inspired since landing in Vegas. She knew Taheim had a lot of connections of his own, but since her connections differed in industry and type from his, she hoped it was sparking some new creative juices.

* * *

"So you and Winter aren't dating?"

Taheim took a sip of his tequila before glancing around to make sure the women were still in the bathroom. "No, we aren't dating."

Rocco gave him a look of disbelief. "Why aren't you dating? You both seem into each other."

Up until now, the conversation had been pretty casual, but he shouldn't have been surprised that Rocco wanted to know about him and Winter. He'd be lying to himself if he said that he wasn't enjoying his time with Rocco and Vanessa. They were definitely a dynamic couple, and every time they looked at each other, Taheim could feel the love between them. On a couple occasions, he had to remind himself that despite how much chemistry he had with Winter, they weren't a couple and he'd accompanied her on this trip only for business.

"Our friends actually set us up on a blind date a few months ago and it was so bad we knew we could never date each other."

Rocco looked around. "So how does two people not dating equate to you both ending up on a trip together? I mean, I know y'all have the fashion show in Chicago that you're working on, but why vacation together if you're just friends?"

"Since we're working together, we had a deal that we would try to be friends. I'm actually surprised at how well we get along considering how bad our first date was." He took another sip of his drink. "Honestly, it's my fault that the date went bad in the first place. She's different from any woman I've met."

"Tell me about it," Rocco said. "I think about the man I used to be and I'm not really sure why Winter befriended me back then. I was a long-haired guitar-playing rocker who didn't care about anything but drinking and getting high."

Taheim looked at Rocco, unable to believe the clean-cut man sitting next to him had been the type of man he'd just described. Rocco was known for his smooth rock music with soft melodies that mingled with sharp chords. He still had a rock edge to him. "How did you meet Winter?"

Rocco smiled. "She had just started college in New York and had snuck into a bar with her friends. I was twenty-one at the time and really didn't give a shit about anyone back then. Mom was a drunk. Dad was in jail. And I was headed down the path of self-destruction. I remember everyone in the bar was dancing to my music except this brown-haired beauty in the back. After the show I asked her why she wasn't dancing and she said that I wasn't really as good as everyone thought I was."

"Sounds like Winter," Taheim said with a laugh.

"She was right, though, man. She saw right through the image I was trying to portray. After a few dates, she said she didn't want to date me anymore, but she did want to be friends and told me that she'd help me get my shit together. To this day, I don't know why I approached her that night or why we remained friends, but years later, I owe her my life. It's because of her that I applied for an internship with a record label and learned the ins and outs of the business, and within four years of meeting her, I was headed to London for a new phase in my career."

Listening to Rocco talk about Winter made him realize just how little he knew about her. He did feel as if he was getting to know Winter, but he didn't know a lot about her past. *Since when do you care about a woman's past?* The question lingered in his mind unanswered. The truth was there, waiting for him to figure it out. But he wasn't quite sure he was ready to hear the answer.

Rocco's voice broke through his thoughts. "On the outside, Winter is strong willed, a go-getter if I've ever seen one. She's fierce in the way she loves those close to her heart, and with what seems like little effort, she can change your entire perspective on how you see things. When I first introduced her to my fiancée, Vanessa hugged Winter harder than I'd ever seen her hug anyone…mainly because she knows I wouldn't be the man I am today and wouldn't have met her in London if it weren't for Winter taking pity on a lost soul."

The words he'd voiced to Winter in his studio came rushing back to him. He'd known Rocco for only a few hours, but if Rocco was being honest, Taheim could be, too. "I'm pretty sure Winter hated me when we first met. But in working together and trying to at least build some type of semblance of a friendship, I told her that I needed to be inspired. Sometime over the past six months, I've felt like I lost my creative spark, and I need to get it back before the Chicago fashion show that we're planning. Everything with us has sort of been a competition and a lot is riding on this masquerade fashion show being a success since it's my brother's grand opening for his new lounge, Inferno."

"If you think Winter's only helping you out because she wants the fashion show to be a success, then you're wrong. Of course she wants the show to be great and your designs to collaborate nicely together. But Winter doesn't just get invested in projects. She gets invested in people."

The ladies returned to the table just as Rocco finished his statement.

"What did we miss?" Winter asked as she took a seat and immediately took a sip of her red wine. *Damn, she's beautiful.* Tonight she wore a black dress that hugged her curves as well as the mint-green dress she'd worn the day before. Her lips today were burgundy, and as always, every movement of her mouth got his undivided attention.

"Do you mind, Taheim?"

That was another thing he liked about her. She genuinely cared about people. He could tell that through meeting her friends Nick, Brian and Rocco, but also, he could tell by how she interacted with the models during practices. Always asking them if they were okay or making sure they didn't just walk the runway, but rather that they understood the vision behind the fashion show. She wasn't just beautiful on the outside. She was beautiful on the inside.

He felt an elbow nudge his arm and turned to find Rocco and Vanessa staring at him with knowing looks in their eyes.

"I'm sorry, what did you say?" he asked, realizing that he didn't know what she was asking him.

She smiled in a way that hit him right in his groin.

"I asked if you wanted to stay for the burlesque performance. Vanessa and I heard it was a great show."

"Oh yeah, sure. That sounds good."

Now all he had to do was sit through the performance and think of anything other than the woman sitting next to him, dominating most of his thoughts.

Chapter 11

Winter glanced at Vanessa and returned her smile. Just as Vanessa had predicted, Taheim couldn't keep his eyes off her. She wanted to pretend as if she weren't enjoying the attention, but there was no use pretending around people who knew her as well as Rocco and Vanessa knew her.

When they had excused themselves to go to the bathroom, Vanessa had wasted no time telling her that she couldn't stop watching the way Taheim was staring at her.

She'd brushed off Vanessa's words, telling her that they were nothing more than friends who happened to be planning a fashion show together. But even as she'd said the words, she'd known they weren't true. There was something brewing between them. Something that she wasn't sure she could ignore anymore.

Now the burlesque performance was about to start and all she could do was hope that the show kept her interest more than the man sitting beside her.

The lights dimmed and a spotlight turned toward the red curtain. There wasn't really a bad viewing spot in the restaurant, but they were sitting at the front tables to the left of the stage with an unobstructed view.

"Ladies and gentlemen, welcome to Madame CeCe's Burlesque Fairy Angels, where all your fantasies come true."

Winter glanced down at her arm at the sudden goose bumps that appeared. *That's strange.* Usually she got them only when she was nervous or uncomfortable about something.

She ignored the goose bumps as the spotlight dimmed and the curtain opened to a man sitting in a chair with a woman on his lap wearing a red corset and ruffled black bottoms. She stood and started dancing seductively in front of him as she talked into the microphone.

"In a land of beauty and enchantment, a clan of pixies reside. But unlike what you've heard in fairy tales, our world is much harder to describe."

The burlesque dancer moved slowly across the stage, her voice reminding Winter of a character in a Disney movie. "We don't fly or cast spells like you mortals believe and we don't use our magic for good. For all those stories and tales you've heard in the books are just fairies who were misunderstood."

The man rose from the chair and went to stand behind her, almost as if he was just there for decoration.

"Have no fear, because tonight we welcome you to our world, so sit back and watch how our secrets unfold… After all, fairies are some of the most delicate of creatures…" She took out her whip and lashed it across the stage. "Or so the story is told."

The lights got brighter and the curtain opened even wider as the man and woman left the stage and more women walked on. She was just starting to get into the show when her goose bumps came back. *Hmm… that's interesting.*

"Is everything okay?" Taheim asked as he placed his hand over the arm she was staring at.

"I'm fine. I just keep getting goose bumps."

"Here, take this." He took off his black blazer and handed it to her. She thought about telling him that she wasn't cold, but it was such a sweet gesture that she curled up into his jacket instead.

"Thanks."

The voices on the stage got their attention.

"Wow, that's some outfit," Vanessa said as the woman who had opened the show returned with a large red feather piece on her head that matched the long feathered skirt she wore with a high slit on the side. It was definitely a showstopper, but what intrigued Winter even more was the way the woman moved across the stage.

The way she swung her hips into a circular shimmy and then cross-stepped into a powerful stance was clever, appealing to the eye and very…*familiar.*

Her heart rate increased while she watched the dancer as flashes of the first time she'd seen this dance crossed her mind. There had been a time when all she'd wanted in the world was to gain the approval of the only person who had ever made her feel as if she were nothing more than a dream-crushing mistake.

Without really thinking about what she was doing, she stood up as the dancer got closer to the side of the stage where their table was located.

She was sure that bright lights restrained the dancer from really getting a good look at the audience, but Winter had seen all she needed to see.

"Why are you standing, sugarplum?" the woman asked flirtatiously.

"You tell me," Winter said sternly. "Maybe it's from the shock of seeing the same dance moves performed onstage that all but took my childhood."

Surprise crossed the woman's face before it was quickly masked. "Winter?"

Winter sighed before running her tongue across her teeth in frustration. "Hello, Mom."

"What are you doing here?" her mother asked, interrupting the show.

"You're the one prancing around onstage and you have the nerve to ask me what I'm doing here?"

As their voices rose a notch or two, the person controlling the lights dimmed them on the side of the stage where Winter and her mother stood.

"We can't do this out here." She looked around the room. "Intermission is about to start. It's fifteen minutes long. Come around back so we can talk in private."

Winter watched her mom leave the stage and tried to comprehend everything that had just happened. When she sat back down, she heard Taheim's voice. "Do you want to go back there and talk to her?"

She looked at him before glancing at Rocco and Vanessa, who also had looks of concern on their faces.

Not exactly how she wanted to end an otherwise great dinner.

"Not really, but I have a few questions that I need answered." Her mother might appear approachable in public, but in private it was a different story.

"How long has it been since you've seen her?" Vanessa asked.

Winter sighed as she looked onstage at the other dancers. "Over three years." *Over three years and I run into her in Vegas?* The irritation running through her veins was enough to make her want to punch something.

Taheim stood and grabbed her hand. "Come on. I'll go with you."

She looked at his hand hesitantly at first. *Let him go with you*, a voice inside her head encouraged. She then stood and followed him to the entrance leading backstage.

"I'll be by your side the entire time unless you want me to leave," he said, offering her comfort, although she doubted he knew to what extent she needed his comfort.

"Thanks," she said softly as the guard—who'd clearly been expecting them—moved aside to let them pass and pointed to another set of swinging doors. When they opened the door to the large dressing room, her mother Sonia was already waiting for them.

"Oh, I didn't know we were allowed to bring our boyfriends to this talk."

Winter glanced at Taheim before looking back at her mother. "So you're in a burlesque show in Vegas and didn't think it was important enough to tell your daughters?"

"Girl, please," she said with a wave of her hand. "You girls never gave a shit about what I did. Only your boring-ass daddy."

"Don't you dare talk about him like that," Winter said defensively.

"Or what?" she said with a laugh. "I forgot how sensitive you were. Where's Autumn and Summer?"

"They aren't here. Not that you really care."

"Oh wee, you're even feistier than the last time I saw you," her mother said as she pulled out a cigarette and lit it with a lighter shaped like a burlesque girl.

"And let's get something straight." She waved her cigarette at Winter. "I run this show. I'm not just a dancer. I became something."

Winter cringed at her words, refusing to let herself go back to a time and place when she would've done anything to please her mom.

"Looks like you finally lost that baby fat."

"I was always satisfied with my size."

"Give me a break, Winter," she said with a laugh. "Who the hell wants to be fat?"

"I was never fat, and even if I had been, not everyone is made to be a size two."

"Only those meant to be somebody. Having you girls may have messed up my figure, but thanks to Dr. Collins, I'm a gorgeous size six."

Even with the makeup, Winter could tell her mom looked slightly different, so she wasn't surprised to learn she'd had plastic surgery. "Being pretty on the outside means nothing if you aren't beautiful on the inside."

Her mom cocked an eyebrow at her as she took another puff of her cigarette. "Says the woman who's spent her entire life in the fashion industry with bougie models."

"Luckily, you taught me how to deal with snobbish people at a young age."

Winter wasn't sure what part of her last statement triggered her mother to look at Taheim, but when her eyes left Winter's and landed on him, inside, she was screaming *Don't look at him!* at the top of her lungs.

"Ain't you that guy I saw on television? The one with that clothing line."

Taheim wrapped his arm around Winter's waist before responding. "Yes, ma'am."

"Well, I'll be damned. You finally snagged you a rich one." She glanced back at Taheim. "And don't call me *ma'am*. That's disrespectful."

Winter threw her hands in the air. "I don't even know why I came back here to try and talk to you. You're the most unreasonable person I know." Winter stepped closer to her mother. "You know what? I pity you. I pity you because you'll spend the rest of your sorry life chasing something that you will never find."

"Oh, my dear pretty girl," her mother said as she stood up from the chair and walked over to them. When she reached them, she brushed her hand through Winter's hair before Winter instinctively pushed her hand away. "Child, they've been saying you were my twin since the day you were born. You look like me. Talked like me until your daddy started taking you around the world, which changed how you spoke and your tone of voice."

She stepped even closer to Winter, but Winter refused to step back and give her the satisfaction of knowing she was getting to her. "Every time you look in the mirror, I want you to remember that I made you. I birthed you. Your sisters may have a few similarities to me, but you're the one who's going to turn out *just like me*."

Winter didn't know what was worse: the fact that after all these years, her mother was still just as nasty toward her, or the fact that Taheim was there to witness it all.

"Winter, your daddy may be a broke-ass painter, but I'm the one who spent hours teaching you how to sew and took you to those classes when you were a kid. So the next time you create one of those little lingerie outfits, just remember… I'm the one who nurtured that talent."

Winter looked her mom dead in the eye. "That's the only thing you *ever* did for me and you never let me forget it."

"You damn right," her mom said as she put out her cigarette. "Hurry back now, kids." She waved her hands for Winter and Taheim to exit the dressing room. "You don't want to miss the end of the show."

As the door slammed in their faces, Winter rushed down the hall into the nearest bathroom. Unshed tears burned her eyes, but she refused to shed one more tear over her mom.

"Are you okay?" Taheim asked as he cracked open the bathroom door and began walking toward her.

"I'm fine," she said as she put up a hand to stop him from getting closer. "But I don't want to cry over her, and if you hug me right now, I won't be able to stop the waterworks."

He stopped his pursuit to her, although she could tell all he wanted to do was hold her.

"Are you okay if we go back to the hotel?" she asked.

Once again, he looked as if he was seconds away from pulling her into a hug, but he withheld himself.

"Let's go."

Chapter 12

Winter had suggested they walk back to the hotel instead of taking a taxi. Taheim didn't mind. He knew she needed to clear her mind.

On their walk, they stopped to watch the water dance at the Bellagio and observed street dancers performing on the sidewalk. Even with the bright Vegas lights, loud music and crowds of people, she was silent during the entire walk.

As they neared the elevator, Taheim wasn't sure if he should offer to walk her back to her room or just maintain the silence and give her space.

He opted to leave the ball in her court. "If you need anything, just call." He didn't like seeing her so distant, and even worse, he didn't like feeling as if he didn't know how to help her.

She looked up at him and searched his eyes. He

wasn't exactly sure what she was looking for, but in that moment, he would have let her search for whatever she needed if it meant wiping that sad look off her face.

"Do you think you can walk me to my room?"

Her voice was so low that he almost didn't hear her. "Of course."

As they boarded the elevator, all he wanted to do was hold her. Despite what she kept telling him, she looked as though she needed a good hug. The walk down the long hallway to her room continued in silence. A quick glance at his watch proved that it had been an hour and a half since the situation had occurred with her mom.

Taheim watched her slip her key card in the door. "Remember what I said. Call me if you need anything."

"I'm not really sleepy," she said, turning the door handle. "Do you want to chat for a while?"

He squinted his eyes in observation. She hadn't said anything for a while, so he doubted they would do much chatting. But seeing the pleading look in her eyes made him not care one iota if they talked the night away or if they remained silent. Even if she just needed him to sit there, he'd do just that.

"So, how do you like your view?" he asked, trying to see if he could get her talking.

"The view is gorgeous," she replied as she kicked off her black heels. "At first I thought a view of the Strip would be awesome. But the minute I walked into the room and saw the mountains in the distance, I couldn't imagine not having that view."

She took out a bottle of red wine from the small refrigerator and poured two glasses.

"Same here." He sat down on the sofa not far from the window. "The Strip is nice, but the mountains are more of an escape from reality."

"Speaking of reality," she said as she handed him a glass of wine and sat next to him on the sofa, "I'm sorry you had to witness that conversation with me and my mother."

"You have nothing to apologize for. You're her daughter—your questions were all valid. I'm just sorry that she didn't reciprocate."

Taking a sip of wine, she brushed off the words. "My mother hasn't been a mother to me or my sisters in an extremely long time and it's really embarrassing that you had to witness that."

"There's nothing for you to be embarrassed about. If anything, your mom should be embarrassed."

"Ha! In order to be embarrassed, she'd have to feel shamed or humiliated by her behavior. But I can assure you, if there is anything I've learned from Sonia Madden Dupree, Miss CeCe or whatever she's calling herself these days, it's that nothing can embarrass her, because she doesn't see her faults."

Taheim had to admit he was a bit shocked by her mother's behavior. It wasn't so much the way she acted but rather the way she spoke to Winter.

"Has your mom always talked like that?"

"If by *like that* you mean rudely and pretentiously, then yes, she's basically been like that my entire life." Winter took another sip of her wine. "In case you didn't notice by the way my mom was looking at you, ever since she divorced my dad and her other husband and stopped seeing the boyfriend who she met while with husband number two, she hasn't dated a man over thirty."

Taheim's eyebrows shot up. "Seriously?"

"Oh yeah. During my junior year of high school, I caught her making out with my boyfriend, who at the time was a senior. When I asked her why she did it, she said she was making sure that he knew how to handle me when I was finally ready to lose my virginity."

Taheim stopped drinking his wine midsip. "You've got to be kidding me."

She let out a forced laugh. "Nope. I'd only seen them making out, but he felt guilty and confessed the next day that they'd been having sex."

What the hell! He was at a loss for words, but he was sure the shocked expression splashed across his face said it all.

"Trust me, I spent many nights waiting for someone to pinch me and tell me that it was all some twisted joke."

"What did your dad say about all this?"

"I never told him about that particular incident. I couldn't bear to hurt his feelings. A couple of months after that, it wasn't an issue anyway, because she'd filed for a divorce. My dad spent years trying to be the businessman my mom wanted him to be. I think he found out when we were kids that my mother had only been interested in his money and the idea that being married to a Frenchman could get her further in her acting or modeling career. Once he'd informed her that one of his paintings had won a prestigious European award and that he was going to pursue his career as an artist, my mom hightailed it out of there so fast the entire day was almost a blur."

"Were your sisters' relationships with your mom just as strained as yours and your dad's?"

"In their own ways, yes. Since I'm the oldest, I was really protective of them. To avoid what was going on, Autumn dived into her studies and Summer really spent a lot of time escaping to friends' houses."

"I can't imagine feeling like that about my mother," Taheim said as he began running his hand up and down her arm. "And you never knew why she treated you differently?"

The look that crossed Winter's face made his protective instinct kick into high gear. Her relationship with her mother had already done its damage, so he couldn't really protect her from that. But he wanted to protect her from the memories. The hurtful memories that were flittering through her mind right now.

"As an adolescent, I was a little on the chubby side. I remember begging my dad to let me sign up for as many sports as I could. In my mind, I figured the more I exercised, the smaller I would be and the more my mother would accept me. Back then I didn't realize that I just wasn't meant to be a stick-skinny kid. I had thighs, a butt, breasts and curves."

Taheim wanted to stop her and tell her that she had the most amazing body that he'd ever seen. That her body had kept him up on more nights than he could count since they had met. No one's definition of beautiful wouldn't include her at the top of the list. But he didn't say any of that. She was opening up to him in a way he somehow sensed she hadn't with others. And for that reason alone, he needed to let her continue.

Winter dropped her head to her glass and began running her finger over the rim. "I spent years listening to her tell me I wasn't pretty enough, would never be beautiful like my sisters and would never turn my dream of being a designer into a reality. Until I finally realized why she didn't love me."

Hearing those words made him wince. *I wonder if she loves so hard because she never felt loved by her mom.* It would probably have had the opposite effect on most people…but not Winter. She had a strength that he had already seen but was slowly beginning to really understand.

"The crazy thing is, she really did introduce me to sewing and I meant what I said—it is probably the only thing in my entire life that she did for me besides bring me into this world. But she didn't teach me to sew for my own benefit. She took me to all those workshops and classes so that I could make her clothes that she would wear for auditions and other things that she never told me about. I didn't only learn she'd been sleeping with my boyfriend my junior year. When I came home early from school one day, I saw her dancing in one of the skimpy outfits she'd had me make for her years before I finally stopped wasting my talent on what she wanted. As I walked closer into our living room, I saw my mom doing that same shimmy I saw onstage earlier today. And the guy sitting in the chair was definitely not my father."

Her voice cracked a little, and just as Taheim's hand was reaching out to touch her face, she stood up from the couch and walked out onto the balcony. His hand dropped back to his side as he thought about her words earlier that day. *If you hug me, I won't be able to stop the waterworks.*

He followed her out onto the balcony and gently ran

his fingers up and down her arms, unable to resist offering her some type of comfort. After a few seconds, she began to lean back on his chest, giving him the opportunity to wrap his arms completely around her. Hugging her felt so right. So natural.

"In case I haven't told you, I think you're an amazing woman." He rested his chin atop her head. "Sometimes people in our lives hurt us in indescribable ways. In your case, your mother never showed you the type of love you needed. But that isn't a reflection of your character. It's a poor reflection of hers. She may never change and I'm glad you're not holding your breath waiting on it. She doesn't define the type of woman you are."

"I know," Winter said with a sigh. "Besides, some children have parents who treat them badly and they never know why they were treated that way. At least I know."

She didn't continue right away and his curiosity began eating away at him. "Why do you think she treats you the way she does?"

"Before my parents divorced, my mom and I had the one conversation in my lifetime where I felt like we truly connected and understood each other. I felt like I was finally seeing a piece of the woman my dad fell in love with. The woman he described to my sisters and me. The woman we never had the fortune of meeting. We'd spent most of the day together and out of nowhere she began laughing so hard that she started crying. At first I didn't understand what was going on, so I began laughing with her until suddenly, she began speaking in between her laughs. So I stopped laughing long enough to listen."

He felt her body tense beneath his arms. "She told me that the reason she called me fat when I was younger was that she knew that I would be prettier than her. My sisters are gorgeous, but they both have a lot of my dad's features. As you saw tonight, I have a lot of hers. Then she told me the reason she said I'd never accomplish my dreams was that she knew I had a talent that she didn't. And probably what hurt the most that night was when she told me that the real reason why she would always hate me was that the day she had me was the day her life changed for the worse. She'd just landed a part in a movie and was so stressed reading over lines that she never noticed she was pregnant until it was too late to get rid of me. When she informed the director, she lost the part."

Winter leaned into him even more. "I knew I shouldn't have been surprised by what she said, but I was. I spent years trying to be the daughter I thought she wanted, needed, even. I learned that night that even if I could do everything she asked me to do, at the end of the day, she felt like I was just like her and she hated me for it. She hated me for being…me."

"You are nothing like that woman." Taheim buried his face in her neck, now understanding the reason her mom had voiced those last words when they were in her dressing room. *She'd say anything to try to break her daughter's spirit.* "Your mom ought to be ashamed of herself for what she put you through. Jealousy is an evil that consumes and can sometimes get the best of people. But that's her problem, not yours."

He turned her around to face him. "Your mom missed out on knowing a terrific woman and having a daughter who I know somewhere in there," he said, pointing to her heart, "still loves her because that's the type of kindhearted person she is. But I hate to say it—she doesn't deserve your love or your sympathy. Your mom has a lot of issues to work through and you can't be the one to help her realize how lost she is. It's time for you to focus on yourself."

He wiped away the few tears rolling down her cheeks. Frustration for what Winter had been through with her mom radiated off his body, blinding him from the chill in the air.

"I'll let you get some rest, but I meant what I said earlier. I'm only a phone call away if you need my help with anything." He turned to walk back into the room, only stopping when he heard her call his name. He turned to where she still stood on the balcony.

She looked at him over her shoulder, her hair whipping across her face in the night breeze. Even after the conversation they'd had, she still looked extremely beautiful. *If you're not careful, you could start to fall for this woman.* Most people knew him for his player-like tendencies, but only those who truly knew him and his past understood why he avoided serious relationships.

"Can you help me now?" Her voice was soft… sweet. She looked so delicate in that moment, and for the tenth time since she'd begun opening up to him, he wanted to go back to the restaurant, find her mom and give her a piece of his mind.

"Sure. What do you need?"

Instead of responding, she walked over to where he stood in the room and placed her hand on the back of his head. With little force, she pushed his head down to hers and stood on tiptoe to place a soft kiss on his lips. For a few seconds, he let her maintain control of the kiss, figuring it was something she needed in that moment. However, her lips began awakening a side of him that had been dormant during their talk due to the seriousness of their conversation.

Both hands went around her waist as he pulled her closer to him. He slipped his tongue between her lips, heightening the kiss to another level. She met the movements of his tongue, surprising him with a few things he didn't see coming. When she moaned into his mouth, he couldn't stop his hands from cupping her cheeks. *Just how I thought they'd feel.* Round. Juicy. Spankable.

He wasn't sure when her feet had left the ground, but before he knew it, he was pinning her against the wall, relishing in the way her legs wrapped perfectly around his waist. Through her moans and his growls, he felt himself slowly lose control, edging closer to the point of no return.

She arched her back, her dress rising higher on her thick maple thighs. *Damn.* He could feel the heat between her legs and he was so hard it was straining against his zipper, threatening to break free. Reluctantly, he stopped the kiss and let her legs drop back to the floor.

"If we don't stop now, I won't be able to control myself."

Instead of the sadness he'd seen in her eyes moments before, he found lust and need. "We just talked about a lot and I would never take advantage of you when you're this vulnerable."

Instead of nodding her head in agreement as he'd expected, she let a sly smile cross her face. *Uh-oh.*

What's that look about? She dropped one hand from his neck and cupped him through his pants. "Taheim, although I really appreciate your concern, I'm a grown woman and you aren't doing anything that I'm not 100 percent on board with. I kissed you first, remember?"

"Of course. But you need to reflect on tonight before we fly out to Hawaii tomorrow. I'm sure tonight has mentally exhausted you."

She averted her eyes from his as the sly smile dropped from her face. "I'll be honest—what happened earlier wasn't exactly how I saw the night going."

She brought both hands to his face. "But right now I don't want to think about my mom or my past or earlier tonight. What I do want is not to be alone tonight. Maybe this will help."

She walked across the room and closed the door leading to the balcony before closing the curtains and dimming the light.

"My mom popping up in Vegas was unexpected, but there is something else that I actually planned just in case."

Her hand went behind her back and Taheim heard the sound of a zipper.

"I wanted to show you something," she said seductively. Unable to stand anymore, Taheim sat in a chair not too far from where she was standing.

"I was inspired to create this the other day after you left my studio." His eyes were glued to her as he watched her slide the straps of her dress off her shoulders, revealing midnight-blue lace. His heart began beating faster in anticipation.

"I call this piece Late-Night Temptation," she said as her dress dropped to the floor.

Taheim let out a curse into the air as he ran his fingers down his face. He'd seen her in lingerie before, but he felt as if he were seeing her for the first time all over. *And she's wearing one of my favorite colors.* Whether it be navy blue, light blue, royal blue, midnight blue…he liked them all.

She seemed to glide toward him, her eyes never leaving his. "Can you stay with me?" she asked when she reached him. She might look confident, but he saw the uncertainty in her eyes. "No more talking. No more reminiscing. Only you and me tonight."

Chapter 13

Her heart was beating out of her chest, and even though she was trying to look confident and sexy, she was so nervous standing in front of him in her lingerie, asking him not to leave.

He stood from the chair and studied her eyes. She understood his concern and she'd probably have felt the same apprehension if the roles were reversed. But she was tired of talking. Fed up with letting her mom control how she lived her life. Tonight Taheim had been there for her in a way no one ever had before. It made her feel important. Understood. *Uninhibited*.

"I don't open up to people easily," she said, leaning into him. "And I want to thank you for listening to me tonight. I never knew how therapeutic it would be."

He looked into her eyes again, only deeper this time. *Goodness*, he looked so sexy. She'd been squeezing her legs together all evening every time she looked at him sitting across the dinner table. As silly as it sounded, dining with her friends had made her feel as if they were a real couple. There were more than a few times she'd wanted to kiss him. Touch him. Just stare into his eyes. *Be careful*, her heart warned. *He doesn't do relationships*. But then again, neither did she.

Suddenly, the look in his eyes changed from concern to desire as he dropped his mouth down to hers and kissed her passionately. His decision had been made. He would stay with her tonight. She felt it in his kiss. Felt it in the way his hands roamed her body. In the way he picked her up just as he had before.

When he placed her on the bed and broke their kiss to look at her again, she smiled and nodded for him to continue, when inwardly, she was doing a happy dance.

Instead of returning to her mouth, his lips brushed against her neck before moving to the swell of her breasts.

"Do you have any idea what seeing you in blue does to me?" he said between kisses. Only when she felt her breasts bounce free did she notice that his hand had unclicked the front of her bra.

"You like the color blue?" she managed to ask breathlessly.

He lifted his head to hers, his eyes unblinking. "It's my favorite color." He sucked a nipple into his mouth. "So you know what you wearing this color means, right?"

His lips made their way down her body, leaving a trail of wet kisses along the way. "What does it mean?" she asked, although she had a pretty good idea.

He answered with his mouth but refrained from

saying words. Instead he deepened his sucks, licks... small precise bites. The way his hands and lips touched her body felt amazing. When he made his way to her panties, she lifted her hips off the bed so he could drag the material off her body.

"Damn." The word left his mouth in a huff of appreciation. Getting naked in front of a man was never something that really bothered her. But she couldn't recall ever being looked at the way that Taheim was looking at her. The way his eyes soaked in every part of her body was actually making her slightly nervous. She lifted her arm to cover herself before Taheim's words made her stop what she was about to do.

"Don't you dare," he said, still observing her body. "Don't you dare cover yourself from me." His eyes met hers and the intensity of his stare made her breath catch. He returned to observing her body, unapologetic in his gaze.

He moved down her body and kissed his way up her calves, but he didn't stop there. His hot tongue scorched the insides of her thighs, causing her hips to buck off the bed. He didn't need to kiss her there for her to feel the effects of his tongue. Just the idea of how close he was to her center almost made her orgasm on the spot.

Suddenly, he stood and began taking off his clothes. "That day I found you half-naked in my bedroom, it took all my energy not to rush over and take you right there...standing up."

She sucked in a deep breath, her eyes fixated on the shirt that he was unbuttoning.

"I knew I couldn't touch you, though. But it wasn't

because of the way we'd met or the blind date that neither of us had enjoyed."

At the last button, he ripped off his shirt, displaying his scored abs and athletic arms. Her eyes didn't
leave his body as she watched him rid himself of his
pants next.

"I knew I couldn't touch you, because the thoughts
I had racing through my mind that day weren't gentlemanly at all. I wanted to take you…long. Hard. Completely. And the need wasn't anything I'd felt before."
His fingers lingered at the rim of his black boxers before he pushed them down to the floor, revealing the
masterful piece of equipment that she couldn't take
her eyes off. "What I felt that night was much more
dangerous because consuming you was all I had on
my mind."

"I knew it," she said, her voice barely above a whis-
per.

"What did you know?" he asked as he kneeled to
the floor.

"I knew you felt it, too, that day in your bedroom.
And I knew that once I saw that—" she pointed to his
erection "—I'd want you to consume me…*all* of me."

At her words, his eyes grew even darker with desire, and in a move she hadn't seen coming, he grabbed
her by the ankles and slid her down the bed until she
was positioned right in front of his mouth.

The minute she felt his tongue dive deep into her
sweetness, she lost all ability to form a coherent
thought. All she could concentrate on was the way
his tongue twirled inside her, eliciting a heightened
desire that she'd never felt before.

"I think I may become obsessed with your taste,"

he said in between licks. *Oh man, if he says anything else, I'm not sure I can hold back.* She'd had oral sex before, and up until now, she'd thought the others had performed just fine. But Taheim was slowly proving that he could not be underestimated. There was a reason why the women in Chicago were fawning all over him. A reason why he'd become so cocky.

She'd gone to a toy party once and all the women had been sharing reasons why they loved being submissive in the bedroom. Winter had been an active participant in each of the conversations up until that point. Up until she realized that she often took control in the bedroom because she didn't like giving any of her power away.

Now, sitting on the edge of the bed with Taheim's tongue moving inside her as if her essence were his sole purpose for living, she knew why she hadn't allowed other men to bring her to a passionate surrender. Why they hadn't been enough.

As in tune to her body as she thought she was, she realized her control wasn't shit against a man who knew how to work his tongue the way Taheim did.

When he cupped his hands behind her ass to pull her closer, her legs spread on their own accord to give him better access. When she felt his hands leave her butt, she met his eyes as he continued to suck her juices.

Watching him pleasure her was an awe-inspiring moment. But what was even more interesting was the look in his eyes as he began pushing her thighs down. It took her only seconds to figure out what he was doing. He was testing her flexibility. She smiled as she dropped her head back to the bed and allowed him to push her legs apart as far as they would go.

When her legs were almost in a split in the air, his tongue increased its movements and her orgasm was running down the court getting ready to land that perfect three-point shot.

"Taheim," she warned when he added two fingers to the already satisfying experience. Within seconds, she exploded in a climax so hard it had her seeing stars, clouds, the sun, the moon and anything else in the sky.

Her stomach quivered at the aftershocks, and when she finally floated back down to earth, she looked up at him still stationed between her legs and stifled a laugh.

"Are you okay?" she asked. He didn't respond but stared at her center.

"It's like unrestrained access to the most intimate part of you."

She finally saw past his surprised look and understood what he was saying. "I do yoga once, sometimes twice a day," she explained as she bit her bottom lip. *He's so cute.* She'd always been flexible, but even she'd admit that she hadn't known her legs could spread that far apart.

He looked from one leg to the other, running his fingers up and down her calves and thighs. When he finally brought his gaze back to hers, the force behind his eyes made her breath catch in her throat. She'd thought she'd seen his desire before, but it was nothing like what she was seeing now. Arousal stirred in her stomach.

"Taheim?" she asked when he remained silent.

He took one more thorough glance of her legs spread wide open before speaking. *Lawd have mercy.* What in the world could he possibly do that was more fulfilling than what he'd just done?

She's going to be the one I can't forget, he thought as he reached down to his pants to grab a condom before he began making his way up the bed. He recalled his dad once telling him and his brother, Ajay, that there would be a time in their lives when they would meet a woman they wouldn't be able to forget. A woman unlike the others and a woman who forced them to reevaluate everything they thought they knew up until that point.

At the time, he'd blown off his father's words. Mainly because he'd just gotten his heart broken by a woman he'd thought he would spend the rest of his life with. A woman who had taught him the true meaning of unfaithful.

Leaning over Winter and seeing the same passion reflected in her eyes that he was sure was in his, he had a feeling that he was about to understand exactly what his father had been trying to tell him.

He positioned himself right in front of her point of entry and brushed a soft kiss on her lips. Her legs spread as his tip began to enter her, welcoming him into her tight, wet heat. She scooted closer to him, the movement bringing him in even deeper.

His eyes rolled in the back of his head as he filled her inch by inch. Their moans mingled with one another and bounced off the walls, no doubt giving the neighbors something to talk about. Not only did Taheim not care that they were loud, he also didn't think they could slow it down if they tried.

Without disconnecting their bodies, he knelt in the bed and brought her on top of him. He assumed that she would just wrap her legs around him. But he was realizing that with Winter, it was best not to assume anything.

She pushed against his chest, forcing him to get off his knees and lie on his back. When she got on top of him, he grabbed her hips, ready to steady her on his cock. In true Winter fashion, she had other plans.

She slid down on top of him so slowly he almost forgot to breathe as he anticipated what she was doing since she was in a squatting position. Then, one leg after the other, she stretched them both out and continued to slide on top of him in a gymnast-type move that he'd never seen before.

"Oh shit," he said when he was buried deep inside her to the hilt. She moved her hips then, using his chest to lift herself off his shaft before bringing herself back down again. Taheim shook his head back and forth, the pleasure too much for him to handle. He briefly glanced at each leg spread out on the sides of his hips and immediately knew that had been the wrong thing to do.

Who the heck was this woman? And how in the world did he get lucky enough to get to know not just the Winter everyone else saw but the Winter she didn't allow everyone to see?

"Winter, I don't know how much longer I can hold on if you keep this move up."

The sneaky smile that crossed her face proved he'd said the wrong thing. With all the strength he could muster, he flipped their positions so that he was on top. He had a feeling he knew her perfect spot and he wanted them both to come.

When she squealed, he knew he had found it. Which was really satisfying, because there was no doubt in his mind that he wouldn't be able to hold on much longer. He took a deep breath, increased his thrusts and continued to work both their bodies into a powerful orgasm.

The glorious sound of Winter gasping into the air and turning to mush in his arms was like music to his ears. He quickly followed with his own release before he collapsed beside her, bringing her on top of him. He wasn't sure why, but he still didn't want to disconnect their bodies yet. And for the first time after sex in years, he wrapped his arms around her and pulled her closer to him. He wanted to embrace her…needed to embrace her.

Chapter 14

Taheim was exhausted, but he had to admit that he was really enjoying seeing Winter in her element. From fashion shows to photo shoots, this woman could do it all. He was impressed that she seemed to do it all with ease.

When they'd finally arrived in Kauai, Hawaii, the day before, they'd made love again and slept the day away in preparation for the photo shoot. When they'd reached the location of the shoot, they'd had to jump right into action. Taheim helped out where he could, but Winter had both hands on deck the minute they arrived.

The location of the shoot was gorgeous, and he'd never been to Kauai, so he appreciated the remoteness the island seemed to offer compared to the Big Island. The luscious green trees, beautiful waterfall and unique birds inhabiting the area were an extremely romantic scene. One that Taheim wished included only him and Winter instead of thirty or so other people involved with the shoot.

He was glad to see that she was really soaking in everything she could from one of the designers on deck who happened to be a close friend of hers, as well as others who'd been in the industry for a while. Although he knew Winter was part French, hearing her have an entire conversation in French with one of the models she'd met earlier had turned him on.

Now the shoot was finally wrapping up. Although models in bikinis and swimsuits still lingered in the area, the only woman who had his nose wide open was the one wearing a light blue sundress that he was sure she was wearing just to drive him crazy with desire.

Just then she looked over to him and smiled in a way that let him know she knew what she was doing. She knew it was extremely difficult not to touch her in public or pull her behind the waterfall and have his way with her.

"You know, I didn't really understand why Winter had agreed to let you tag along on her trip," said Chris Wright, Winter's friend, who was a swimsuit designer and fashion photographer. "But now I get it."

He didn't miss the knowing look in Chris's eyes. When Winter had told him about Chris, he had assumed he was another male friend from her past. He hadn't expected to see a woman with brown-and-blond-streaked hair, hazel eyes and a slight Southern accent. Then he'd learned that they'd been college roommates for two years and had maintained contact after graduation.

"What do you understand?" he asked, turning his gaze back to Winter.

"Well, for starters, she said you both were just friends. But there's nothing friendly about the way you've been looking at her all day."

Taheim laughed. No point denying it. "Is it that obvious?"

"Hmm, only to everyone who was at this shoot today," she said with a laugh. "But I can tell she likes you just as much, so no worries."

Taheim liked Chris. She'd made it a point to check on him throughout the day to make sure he was okay. In fact, he'd liked every friend of Winter's he'd met on this trip.

"She really is something special," he said honestly. "And she has a good group of friends."

"Even Nick and Brian?" she asked with a laugh. One glance at Chris and he knew she had somehow found out about his lingerie theater performance in Vegas.

He laughed as he shook his head. "I should have known Winter wouldn't keep that a secret."

"Oh no, she didn't say anything. Nick and Brian called me right after. They knew I would meet you in a couple days."

"Wow, they didn't waste any time." He watched Winter walk over to a few other models and give them hugs. "I liked Nick and Brian, but I don't think I have a future on Broadway."

"That's not what Brian said." Her eyebrows suggested he'd said quite a bit.

"I don't even want to know."

He watched one of the other models pull Winter in

for a selfie that eventually led to all the models gathering around to take pictures with her.

"For what it's worth, I think that you two would be pretty good together if you gave a real relationship a shot."

He glanced back at Chris. "I'm sure Winter told you that I'm not good with relationships."

"Why's that?"

He stopped his face from curling up into a frown. "I just know."

From the inquisitive look in her eyes, he could tell she wanted to ask him more questions, but she didn't. Talking to her was a reminder that although he'd recently learned a lot about Winter and the past experiences that made her the woman she was today, he hadn't opened up to her yet. He hadn't explained why he knew he was bad in serious relationships and the reason he'd developed his playboy-like ways.

The words she'd texted him a couple weeks ago echoed in his mind… *You're still cocky as hell. But underneath all that is a man with a story. Hopefully I'll hear it one day.*

"Well, it was nice meeting you," Chris said, breaking through his thoughts. That was when he noticed Winter was walking toward them. "Word of advice. Open up to her. She's one of the most understanding people I know. Only a dumbass could miss that fact."

Taheim just smiled at Chris.

"It was nice meeting you, too, Chris," he said as he gave her a look that he hoped proved to her that he understood exactly what she meant. He'd already decided that it was long overdue. He had to tell Winter exactly why he was the way he was.

* * *

Winter glanced over at Taheim as they sat on the patio, having just finished a delicious dinner. The plan had been to go to an amazing restaurant on the resort grounds not far from their villa, but the current rainstorm had forced them to eat outside on the covered patio instead.

It had been nice to have an intimate dinner and listen to the rainfall, but Taheim was quieter than she'd ever seen him before and she wasn't sure why.

"Would you have preferred that we stay in separate villas?" she asked when he seemed more interested in the ice slowly melting in his glass than having a conversation with her. "Because I'm sure we can still arrange that."

He looked up as if he were hearing her speak for the first time, proof that he hadn't really been listening to her during dinner.

"Is everything okay?" she asked instead of repeating her question.

"I definitely don't need my own villa," he stated. "I'd never pass on the opportunity to have you close by me."

She studied his eyes, unsure of the change in his personality. "What's wrong?" Her voice was pleading even to her own ears.

He sighed before responding. "I'm terrible at relationships."

She blinked. "Um, okay. I admit the sex was amazing, but I never asked you for a relationship."

"Wait a minute. Scratch that." He waved his arm and sat upright in his chair. "What I meant to say is that the first time we met—that blind date that I was extremely late for? I had a reason. Not a good one, but still a reason."

"What happened?"

He clasped his hands in front of him on the table. "My ex had called me to tell me she was divorcing her husband. Which wouldn't concern me, except I heard that her husband hadn't been the nicest person to her during their marriage."

"I'm sorry to hear that," she said sincerely.

"I was, too. My ex and I met in high school and had been attached at the hip. We were that couple, you know, the one that everyone says is going to be together forever."

"Did you break up during college?"

"I wish. It would have saved me years of wasting my time and I could have really dated around in college and seen what else was out there." Taheim stood to walk to the minibar pair on the patio to replenish his drink. "We dated all through college and a few years after. We were engaged for a few months before I caught her at our home with one of my guy friends at the time. He was a real jerk with the ladies, but my friend and business partner Jaleen and I played basketball with him in high school, so we still hung out, like most guys on the team did."

"That's awful." When thinking about Taheim, Winter had tried not to assume too much, but she'd suspected a woman had done him wrong.

"That's why you got so upset on our blind date when I said those things to you about a woman hurting you so badly you developed this playboy alter ego."

"You were right, and yeah, that was why I got so pissed off."

"Oh man," she said placing her hand on her forehead as she thought about what else she had said. "And I called you damaged goods, too. I am so sorry."

Taheim sat back down across from Winter. "You definitely caught me off guard, but I took the frustration of my ex's phone call out on you, and for that, I'm sorry, too."

He turned to glance out into the darkness as the rain continued to fall. "When you were telling me about your mother, it brought me back to my time with Andrea. That's her name."

"How so?"

"Well, when I dated Andrea, there was nothing I wouldn't do for that girl. I may be somewhat of a playboy now, but I would never *ever* cheat on a girlfriend or someone I'm dating seriously. Which is why I'm up-front with the women I get into bed with."

It briefly crossed her mind that she didn't recall having a conversation about the rules, those guidelines that you followed for casual sex. Winter wasn't even a casual sex–type girl, so she definitely didn't know how to approach the topic with Taheim.

"The fact that they had been sleeping around for years…that I'd been sharing the one woman I wanted to marry with another man, put me in a bad head space for a while. Until my family and close friends told me Andrea was never worth the trouble anyway."

"Sometimes it's hard to see what others see." She understood that more than most.

"It really is. I felt like while we were dating, no one ever said anything bad about her. They may have alluded to some things, but I didn't find out how bad people thought she was for me until after I broke off the engagement. Looking back, I know the only reason I changed the type of person I was to fit the type of man she wanted me to be was that I'd been there for her hard times. I was the one who she called when her stepdad came home drunk and became volatile to her and her mom. And I was the one who she called when she got the call that her older brother had been killed in Iraq."

Winter nodded her head, understanding a few more things about him now. "That's understandable. You helped her through so much. You were blinded by what you wanted to do to help her."

"Kaya once told me it was called hero syndrome," he said, laughing for the first time all night.

Gosh, I didn't know how much I missed hearing him laugh. "Kaya's right. And by the way, you comforted me when I talked about my mom. I can see that side of you."

"You're mistaken," he said, shaking his head. "That side of me died a long time ago. With you, I was there because I wanted you to know that even though you have your dad and sisters, there's at least one other person who understands your struggle. One person who admires the person you are…inside and out. I wanted to save Andrea because she needed saving." His eyes met hers. "You're one of the strongest women I've ever met. You got through all the tough stuff. You just need a friend."

Her breath caught at the sincerity of his words. "Thanks, but you can't just associate wanting to be someone's hero with Andrea. It's a part of you, no matter if you try and hide it or not. There's nothing wrong with wanting to be someone's everything." She leaned closer to make sure he heard her words. "You and I have something in common in the sense that we've both let our toxic relationships define a part of who we are. It's okay to allow experiences to make you stronger. But the minute we let our insecurities take precedent over everything else is the minute we have to reevaluate our purpose."

"You're right. I didn't notice how much we did have that in common. I gave Andrea so much of me…all I had to give at the time. For ten years, I was consumed by her and the idea that no matter how hard I tried, I still wasn't enough for her."

You're enough for me. She gasped at the direction of her thoughts. *Wait, what?* They'd been together non-stop for days, but that was no excuse to become delusional.

"Are you okay?" he asked in concern.

"Yes, I'm fine." She brushed away her thoughts. "Did she ever tell you why she cheated?"

Taheim huffed. "She said she'd gotten bored and that I hadn't matured into the man she wanted me to be."

"So giving her your heart and promising to love her forever wasn't enough," she said as a statement rather than a question. "That's a sorry excuse and you're anything but boring."

"Thanks," he said, pinning her with a sexy look she'd missed since they had started talking about Andrea.

It was hearing stories like this that really irritated Winter. Stories about a selfish woman who hurt a good man and made it worse for all those who came after. "You put your faith in her and she took your love for granted. You know I understand. Did she say something to upset you the day we went on our date?"

"Over the past year or so, Andrea has been calling me or leaving me messages about how much she misses me and how she made a mistake leaving me for her husband. But she didn't give a shit about my feelings when I debuted Collegiate Life to the world and she went to the tabloids and told them that she was my one true love and all this other BS."

Winter took a sip of her drink as a few unchoice words popped through her head at the type of woman Andrea was. "She's got some nerve."

"That's Andrea. Conniving, deceitful and, unfortunately, believable at times. She had the media eating out of the palm of her hand, and before I knew it, some online magazine published an article about our relationship, her infidelity and so much more. It's not like people in high school didn't know our story, so the magazine could have gotten the scoop from anywhere. But I know Andrea had a hand in it."

Winter disliked Andrea more and more by the second.

"She'd moved to Texas with her ex and she called the day of our date to tell me she would be in Chicago the entire month of December and was thinking about moving back permanently. But that wasn't even the worst part about her call."

"What was the worst part?" she asked when he didn't continue.

"The fact that she told me if I didn't see her, she would go to the tabloids before the debut of T.R. Night and really give them something to talk about."

Winter scrunched her forehead in confusion. "What

could she possibly have to tell them? Y'all have been broken up for years."

Taheim observed her through cautious eyes, as if he was trying to decide how to tell her something.

"She didn't say and hung up when I asked. Now that it's been a while since the call, I made a call of my own before we left for Vegas, so I think I know what she's planning."

"And what might that be?" she asked in a lower voice for no reason other than the fact that she was a little nervous about what he might say.

"She's probably going to try and claim that I'm the father of her eight-year-old son."

Chapter 15

Don't look shocked. Don't look shocked. Big fail. From the way his eyes observed hers, she was pretty sure she looked stunned.

"Is there a possibility that he's yours?" she asked when she found her voice.

"I honestly don't know," he said, taking another sip of his drink. "I never even knew she had a son, nor did the friends she still had back in Chicago. After that call, something told me to go on Facebook, find her ex-husband and reach out to him. When I did, he told me good luck dealing with her and that after I had broken off the engagement and they'd moved to Texas, she had claimed she had a trip out of the country and was gone for almost a year."

"Let me guess," Winter said, crossing her arms over her chest. "She lied about the work trip and was giving birth to her son instead."

"Bingo. Apparently, when she got back, they got married and that was it. Then eight months ago, her ex-husband was in Florida on business and ran into Andrea's mother, who had moved there after her step-dad passed. Her mother had a little boy by her side. After he cornered Andrea and her mother about it, they confessed. All those years, he had thought they couldn't visit Andrea's mom because their relation-ship was strained…"

"The real reason was that her mom was raising her son and she didn't want her husband to find out," Winter continued for him, unable to process the spi-ral effect of this story. "That's the most ridiculous thing I've ever heard, which is crazy considering the things I just told you I witnessed from my own mother."

Winter scrunched her face in thought. "Better yet, I take that back. It's right up there with the crazy crap my mom would pull."

His mouth curled into a smile, but he looked a thou-sand miles away.

"Did her ex tell you that he thought the child was yours?"

Taheim was already nodding his head. "He had a paternity test done and he wasn't his. The week after he got the results, he filed for divorce."

"So they didn't get a divorce because her ex-husband was mean?"

"After talking to him, I don't think so. But remem-bering how he used to be with other girls he had dated, it's still possible."

She racked her brain to try to find the right words to say. Feeling bold and wanting to change the mood, she stood and walked over to him and sat on his lap. He immediately wrapped his arms around her, and just like that, her heart began to beat a little faster than before.

"We all have problems. We all have stuff we have to work through. But you've spent your high school years, college years and a few years after college dealing with Andrea and her issues. I know it's only been a week since you talked to her ex, but have you decided if you want a paternity test?"

"Yes, and if he is my son, I plan on being in his life. I can't even believe that she wouldn't tell me something so important."

Winter smiled as her hand cupped his cheek. "You're a good man. A responsible man. Don't let her take anything else from you. I think it's great that you're going to address the situation and get a paternity test. And whatever doubts you have about yourself or the type of man you are in a relationship, you need to just forget."

Some of the tension in his features relaxed at her words and she enjoyed the fact that she was the one to bring him relief.

"Haven't you noticed?" he said as his lips curled into a smile. "I attract crazies. Andrea wasn't the only one. I tried to seriously date after her and that woman was insane, too."

Winter scrunched her face. "Hmm, I was going to ask you to explain, but then I thought about that incident in the restaurant with the woman who interrupted our terrible date and made it even worse."

"Ah," he said, pointing a finger into the air. "Amanda. Yeah, that was the last time I saw her."

She didn't hide the smile that crossed her face. "Hope I wasn't the one who ruined that. Even though she was the one who was trying to hijack my date, wearing way too much perfume and acrylic nails that I'm sure were strong enough to scratch the paint off your car if you pissed her off."

He laughed so hard his whole body shook, and since she was on his lap, hers shook along with his. "Believe it or not," he said as his laughter settled and his face grew more serious, "it was definitely because of you, which reminds me…"

With skill and ease, he slightly lifted up from his seat to reach in his back pocket, careful not to let her slip from his lap. "Here's the fifty bucks I owe you."

"You are so bad," she said with a laugh as she brushed his hand away. "So I was right. All the women you dated weren't top quality like you said."

"Ehh." He waved his free hand back and forth. "Naw, not really."

"Then I don't need the money. Beating you in a bet is satisfaction enough."

They both laughed and Winter noted that the noise in the background was growing louder.

"Looks like it's raining harder." When he didn't respond, she looked down at him.

"Thank you," he said when her eyes met his.

"For what?"

He brushed a few strands of fallen hair out of her face. "Thank you for letting me accompany you on this trip and introducing me to your great group of friends, but more important, thank you for listening to my story and not passing judgment."

Winter had never considered herself an emotional person, but seeing the honesty reflected in his eyes tugged at emotions she'd never felt before.

"Then I should be thanking you for the same thing." She let her hand rest on his chest. "And I'm really glad that you came on this trip with me."

She felt his hands roam up and down her back before rising to her neck and gently connecting their lips in a tender kiss that literally stole her breath.

He was an expert at kissing, among other things. Or maybe it was just combustible when they kissed each other? Maybe it was their connection, this indescribable bond. This insatiable chemistry between them that seemed to grow the more time they spent together.

"Winter, I changed my mind. I don't think this is a good idea."

Taheim was always up for trying new things. Given that those new things fit into the comfortable box of things he would actually do. Better yet, the more he thought about it, the more he realized that in actuality, there were thousands of things he wouldn't actually try to do. And jumping off a rocky cliff was one of them.

"You'll be fine, Taheim. What's the worst that can happen?"

His head whipped so fast to face her the movement made her jump. "What do you mean, what's the worst that could happen? How about I jump off this cliff, hit a rock, get caught in a current and drown."

"Oh, come on," she said as she yanked his arm. "Look at those lush green trees in the distance on that small piece of land that we can only get to by swimming. And that beautiful turquoise-blue sea that is completely calm. Even the tropical birds flying above us agree that we should jump. And when we do, we can release all our problems, all of our worries. Leave our minds blank to only soak in this gorgeous scenery. This perfect moment."

He wasn't sure if it was the fact that her hair was braided in pigtails, that her arms were outstretched to the sky or that he could possibly plummet to his death that made him leery of the entire cliff-diving experience. But it was probably a combination of all three. And Winter's free-spirit, throw-your-inhibitions-to-the-wind personality wasn't helping the situation.

"Look, flower child," he said, trying to bring her back to reality. "We can see those lush green trees from the ground just fine. I'm pretty sure we could rent a kayak or canoe to get to that island instead of swimming in shark-infested water. The sea may look beautiful and calm, but do you even know how deep it is or what things are living in water that deep? And I can assure you that jumping off a cliff will not calm me. If anything, I could have a heart attack before I even hit the water."

"Dramatic much!" she said as she placed her hands on her hips. "When I mentioned that I wanted to go on a hike today and dive into the ocean, why did you agree to come with me?"

Flashes of their bodies intertwined in the crisp white sheets crossed his mind. The light breeze from the open patio door cooling off their hot bodies. Her breasts pressed against his chest, thighs to thighs.

"I don't even know why I asked," she said with a laugh. "It's obviously written all across your face."

After the conversation they'd had the other night about his ex, they'd spent the whole night feasting on each other just to wake up the next morning and do it again. Yesterday afternoon and evening had been dedicated to what he'd wanted to do in Hawaii. Today was Winter's choice. So far, he'd already woken up at an ungodly hour, hiked up a hill, and eaten two bananas and a granola bar when all he wanted was some real food. Now she was trying to convince him that jumping off a cliff could be a liberating experience.

"If you do this for me, I'll make it worth your while." She leaned up on tiptoe and planted a soft kiss on his lips, slipping him a little tongue. It was useless to resist her. He'd already bared his secrets. Exposed his insecurities as she soothed the hurt.

"How do you do that?"

"Do what?"

"Undress me layer by layer, leaving me naked and exposed."

She crooked an eyebrow at him. "Are we talking about last night or is that a metaphor?"

"It's a metaphor."

She giggled. "In that case, I don't know. But I can tell you that you're not alone. You have the same effect on me. The ability to make me open up in ways I never have before. Which is why I'm trying to convince you to jump off this cliff."

She glanced over the side of the cliff at the water, excitement evident in her features. "Trust me. You'll be glad you did it."

He walked over to her and followed her line of vision. "What the hell is that?"

"Calm down," she said with a laugh. "They're just dolphins."

"Oh, only dolphins," he said sarcastically as he waved his hands in the air.

"You'll be fine. Dolphins are friendly."

"Up here, they look small. But I bet they're much bigger when you're swimming right beside them."

"The average dolphin is about eight feet long. That's not that big."

He gave her a look of disbelief, but she didn't seem fazed by his uncertainty. There were really only two options and neither appealed to him at the moment. One, tell Winter that there was absolutely no way he was jumping off a rocky cliff and know she'd understand. Two, jump off a cliff, which would be one of the most terrifying things he'd ever done. The first option would result in a disappointed Winter. And maybe she was right. Maybe he would have some type of aha moment. The second option—the one he couldn't believe he was contemplating—was frightening, but some would say that being an entrepreneur and following your dreams no matter who doubted your capabilities was just as terrifying and he'd done that just fine.

Mind made up, he nodded his head in agreement, barely able to laugh at her jump for joy because his brain was too busy trying to figure out how far out he should jump.

"Do you see that section in the water right there?" He followed the direction of her hand.

"Yes."

"That's where we have to jump."

"Okay, are we jumping one at a time?"

"We can jump together, but I'm jumping a couple feet away from the section I just pointed at for you."

She took a few steps back. "Are you ready? We're going to run and jump. No thinking. Just do it."

He jumped in place and waved out his arms as he would to loosen up before he took the court in a basketball game.

"I'm ready," he said, nodding to her. She smiled as she leaned down to prepare to run. He followed suit.

"Ready. Set. Go." She took off running slightly before him. *Don't think. Just do it. Don't think. Just do it. You got this. You. Got. This.* When he reached the cliff's edge, he cleared his mind of fears, finally understanding that this was a once-in-a-lifetime experience.

As he learned the true meaning of gravity, he was surprised that the thought that crossed his mind wasn't about his clothing line. It wasn't about his nightwear line. He wasn't thinking about his family or friends and definitely not about Andrea. The only thought he had was about Winter. The woman who'd somehow impacted his life more than anyone before and made him believe in taking chances with the opposite sex. Something he'd lost sight of over the years.

It took only seconds for his body to hit the water. When his head peeked above the surface, Winter was there. Wearing a big smile on her face. However, what captivated him the most about the moment wasn't her smile or the gleam in her eye that proved she was proud of him. It was the fact that without even asking, she'd known what he needed. A lot of people in his life considered him fearless, which he'd admit he liked. But with Winter, he didn't have to pretend or always be courageous in his efforts. He just had to be himself and she made him feel as if that was just fine.

Chapter 16

The swim to the small island was a little longer than Winter had anticipated, and by the look on Taheim's face, he was just as winded as she was. Luckily, when they finally made it to shore, they were excited to find a small hut that offered towels and other souvenirs for purchase. A boat of tourists had also arrived and were eating an authentic Hawaiian lunch on the beach. They blended in perfectly.

"I'm stuffed." Taheim spread out on the towel and rubbed his stomach.

"Me too." She glanced around and noticed a path that she was sure led to another part of the island, as the concierge at the hotel had informed her earlier that morning. "Hey, before you get too cozy on this sand, follow me."

He smiled and shook his head. "I should have

known you had other plans. I heard that the boat heads back to the mainland in two hours. We'll be back by then, right?"

"Oh yes," she said, standing and grabbing their towels since their discarded clothes were still atop the cliff. "I can't swim back after eating all that food."

Luckily, they hadn't brought anything valuable with them. What they did have, a waterproof watch and some cash, was as dry as ever thanks to the waterproof case that had easily slid into Taheim's swim trunks.

After about twenty minutes of walking, Winter finally found the area she'd heard about. She walked down the narrow path, pushing aside elongated green leaves as she hiked. A few more steps and they reached the teal water and intimate waterfall stationed in between two rock formations.

"Wow," Taheim said behind her. "This is beautiful."

"According to the woman at the information desk at the hotel, it's one of the most romantic areas on this island."

"You don't say." His arms curled around her waist and he placed a soft kiss on her neck. It always surprised her how soft his lips were. Every kiss he placed on her body made her feel as though she were being draped in silk or velvet.

She leaned her head against his chest. "You know what I want to do?"

He continued to place kisses along her neck, moving to the spot right behind her ear that he'd learned made her quiver in desire. "What do you want to do?"

"See what's behind that waterfall."

His eyes followed the direction of her hands. "Let's check it out," he said with a laugh.

A quick survey of the area proved that the only way to get on the other side of the waterfall was getting into the water. They placed their towels on the ground and paddled into the water.

She was all set to enter first, but Taheim grabbed her hand and pulled her behind him. "This waterfall doesn't look too big, so we should be able to go underneath along the edges. I'll go under first and pull you through."

"I thought you didn't like deep water, because you can't see the bottom."

"Have you seen this water?" he asked. "It's so gorgeous and so clear I can see right to the bottom."

He was right. The water really was crystal clear. "Okay," she said softly, loving the way he was taking charge. She didn't have the heart to tell him she'd been on the swim team in high school and had visited more waterfalls in her lifetime than she could count. It was so funny that she used to think his ways were a bit bossy and arrogant. Now she thought them to be endearing and attractive.

When they could no longer touch the ground, they swam side by side. Just as he'd said, he went to the edge of the waterfall and swam underneath. She waited a few seconds, and when she heard his faint voice, she poked her head closer to the waterfall. His hand reached through the water and she yelped as he pulled her through.

"Oh, wow," she said as she looked around the small cave, noticing the dark rocks surrounding them and underneath them. "We can actually stand up."

"We sure can." He pulled her to him and crashed his lips to hers. The unique rock formation was quickly

forgotten as her tongue played with his in a seductive
game of hide-and-go-seek.

He backed her into the rocky wall and she noticed
that the water was shallower there.

"I've always had a fantasy that involved a waterfall," she said as she lightly ran her fingers over his
chest. His heartbeat quickened underneath her hand.

"Do you want to know what it is?"

He nodded his head but still didn't say anything.
She loved the expression on his face. The anticipation. The power she had over him and the way he
made her want to do things she'd never dared to do
with other men.

"I'll give you a hint," she said as she licked her lips.
"It involves my tongue."

His eyes darkened and she took that opportunity
to change their positions so that his back was against
the wall instead.

"And my lips." She placed soft kisses across his
neck and chest, paying close attention to the spot that
made his toes curl. The spot that she'd learned late
last night could bring him to the edge quicker than
anything else.

"You're not playing fair," he breathed. "If you keep
your lips on that spot, whatever you're trying to do
won't last long."

Little did he know she was sure he wouldn't last
long with what she planned to do next. Her lips tingled
from the salt water as she continued to kiss his body.

"Did you know I was on the swim team in high
school?"

He blinked a couple times before his eyes roamed
over her body. "No, I didn't. But judging by how great

you look in that white-and-pink bathing suit, I'm not surprised."

"I was on the team for all four years," she said, wearing a sly smile. "And do you know what I learned in those four years?"

He squinted his eyes in confusion. "What did you learn?"

She stood on her tiptoes, careful not to slip on the rock beneath her, and brought her mouth close to his ear. "I learned how to hold my breath on average for one minute and forty seconds."

She watched him swallow. Hard. While he was still processing what she was saying, she bent down and prayed that she could master the ability of breathing and pleasing at the same time.

She slipped her hand in his swim trucks and cupped him until his erection was exactly where she wanted it to be. He leaned his head against the wall and blew out a long breath. Taking a deep breath of her own, she dipped her head under the water and placed her mouth on his tip before sucking him in as much as her mouth would allow.

She could feel some of the water getting in her mouth, so she relaxed her throat muscles as much as she could and concentrated on her main goal…bringing Taheim to a pleasurable new level while living out one of her fantasies.

She lifted her head to get some air. "Did I forget to mention that I didn't have this particular fantasy until I saw that waterfall during the photo shoot and then saw you watching me? All those women were around, half-naked, but you only watched me. The look you had in your eyes made me want to make love to you right then and there. But not with our bodies…with my tongue."

She dipped her head back underwater and braced her hands on the rock wall behind him. *Time to really put those breathing lessons during swim class to use.* As her mouth went to work, she inwardly smiled at the animalistic noises echoing throughout the cave.

Taheim shook his head back and forth, feeling more of his control slip the longer Winter's head remained underwater. He didn't know how long she had been down there, and he would have been worried if he didn't feel her tongue gliding up and down his shaft.

It took a while before he realized that the noises in the cozy cave were coming from his own mouth. But now the voices he heard weren't really sounding like his. He glanced at the waterfall and saw shadows on the other side. *Crap, it looks like people.*

"Winter," he said with all the strength he could muster. Instead of bringing her head above the water, she increased the movement of her tongue.

"Holy shhh—" *Okay, so maybe saying her name is the wrong way to go about this.*

He opened his mouth to form another sentence, but all that came out were broken words. He could barely formulate his thoughts with her triple-working him into submission, let alone say any comprehensible words out loud. He tried again.

"People," he said just as she alternated fondling his balls from the left to the right one.

"There." *Oh man.* Now she was doing some type of twirling rotation.

"People. There. Now. Winter." *Finally, I said it.* Only

she wasn't stopping, and within seconds, he was to the point of no return. He couldn't hold back any longer. In a few moments, he knew he would come harder than he ever had before. Then again, what man would be able to last long with a gorgeous woman pleasing him below in such an exotic location? Odds were, none could.

So he didn't try. When he came, the growl he released into the cave was loud. Forceful. Powerful. He heard yelps from the people on the other side of the waterfall, but he didn't give a damn. Not right now. Not in this moment.

He was still banging his fists against the rock wall in satisfaction when Winter arose from the water looking like a vision plucked from every man's hottest fantasy.

He wanted to say something. Express how amazing it was for him. But he didn't want to say anything cheesy like *Thanks for rocking my world* or *You did a good job, kid.* What Winter had just done wasn't something he would ever forget. Could ever forget. Because she wasn't the type of woman a man forgot about. Everything about her was branded in his soul, and although the notion should have scared the shit out of him, it didn't. If anything, it made him want to hold her tight and never let go. Instead of saying anything, he kissed her. Hard. Passionately. Completely. Until he heard voices, though he couldn't make out what type of language they were speaking.

"What's that?" Winter asked.

"Um, while you were underwater, we got company."

Her eyes grew big and her hand flew to her mouth. "You're kidding me."

"Wish I was." He grabbed her arm. "Let's get out of here."

The minute they crossed to the other side of the waterfall, Taheim realized they had caused a little more commotion than they'd thought. It seemed they'd really frightened a few tourists. Five pairs of eyes watched them walk ashore, each displaying a different emotion.

The young guy who Taheim assumed worked on the island gave Winter an assessing look before shooting Taheim two thumbs-up. A mother grabbed her child to cover his eyes, even though they were both wearing swimwear, and gave them a disapproving look. The father eyed Taheim with envy, no doubt jealous that he hadn't been on the receiving end of any of the pleasure that had occurred behind the waterfall. And the grandmother shocked Taheim the most of all. She was snapping pictures of them the entire time they walked out of the water, and when they passed her, she reached out her hand to give them each a high five.

They grabbed their towels and hightailed it out of there, both of them laughing hysterically when they were in the clear.

"Oh my God, I can't believe they heard you." She slapped him on the arm.

"Ouch," he yelled. "It's your fault. You shouldn't have been so good."

She shook her head, still laughing. "And what about that grandma? I hope we don't show up on some random online family photo album."

"I'm not sure," Taheim said, shaking his head. "Grandma seemed a little freaky, so I think we need to be more worried about showing up on some random porn site. Now that I remember, I did see lights flashing on the other side of the waterfall when we were in the cave. And that camera was waterproof."

They both briefly stopped laughing and looked at each other. At the sound of a clicking noise behind them, they both turned and saw the grandma waving as she continued to take pictures of them. Just like that, they were back to laughing hysterically.

Chapter 17

"Okay, people, that wraps up today's practice. The fashion show is next Saturday. That's only one week away. I will email each of you the information for the final practice before the show."

Winter began organizing the chairs in Inferno, unable to resist stealing a glance in Taheim's direction as she did. Just as she'd hoped, he was already waiting for their eyes to meet. He looked her up and down, and just like that, her entire body went hot.

When they'd arrived back in Chicago last week, they'd both been immediately thrust back into their lives. Decisions had to be made. Documents had to be signed. Practice for the fashion show had to be held. Designs had to be finalized.

Despite the craziness of their everyday lives, at night it was all about them. It was all about trying to hold on to that cocoon they'd both been in while they were in Vegas and Hawaii.

"Seriously, Winter?"

She whipped her head at the sound of her sister's voice. "What?"

Autumn crossed her arms over her chest. "On a scale of one to ten, how close are we?"

"Ten."

"Do I have the highest IQ out of everyone you know?"

"Unfortunately, yes," she said with a laugh.

"And I trust you with my secrets."

"I know," Winter said with a shrug.

"And you trust me with yours?"

"Of course!"

Autumn walked a little closer so that the people around them couldn't hear. "So how in the world can you lie to me about you and Taheim having sex?"

Winter blinked a couple times. "Um, I don't know what you're talking about."

When they were on the flight back to Chicago, they'd agreed not to tell their friends about what had happened while they were away. To be honest, it had been her decision. Her sisters weren't used to her being in a relationship, but even worse, she wasn't used to being in a relationship. Taheim had alluded to the fact that he didn't want to date any other women but her, and she had told him that she felt the same way. But at the end of the day, she was nervous and wasn't quite sure why she was so scared.

Actually, she was pretty sure she was scared because of how much she liked him and how quickly their relationship had turned from enemies to sort-of friends to lovers to a couple. She couldn't process it all, so she'd asked him if they could keep it a secret until after the fashion show. She'd blamed it on the fact that doing so would help them maintain a professional relationship in the public's eye, when in reality, she needed more time to get used to the idea of being in a relationship with Taheim.

Taheim. She still couldn't believe how much their relationship had changed in seven days. Or how much they'd learned about one another. He'd even pulled two all-nighters designing pieces for the fashion show since he'd finally found enough inspiration to finish his debut collection. He'd also added a few holiday pieces into the mix. All in all, the trip had been a success and she was so glad they'd shared some of those experiences together.

Even looking at him now, she could tell that he was exhausted, but the fire in his eyes held a promise. An assurance that no matter how tired he was, there was no way he was letting her go home tonight alone. She could have looked at him forever, but an irritating sound caused her to avert her eyes.

"Three fifty-eight, 359, 360. Oh, hi, Winter," Autumn said with a small wave. "My name is Autumn and I am your very perceptive, definitely not gullible, Irish-twin mind-reading, went-to-your-house-two-nights-in-a-row-just-to-prove-my-point sister. It's nice to see that you can stare at Taheim like you're ready to rip his clothes off for six minutes straight and still think that everyone in this room is oblivious to the fact that you guys hooked up in Vegas. Or Hawaii. But probably both places."

Whoops! Busted. "A little in Vegas, but mainly

Hawaii," she finally confessed. "I told you about Mom, right?"

"Don't change the subject. You told me about Mom twice already and I know you hate talking about her, as do I. You brought her up because my asking about Taheim forces you to own up to your relationship with him."

"We haven't put labels on anything."

Autumn glanced at Taheim, then back to Winter. "News flash, sis. That man has been staking his claim on you since you both got back. Word is, he has his eye on you and has no plans of letting another man get within a few feet of you unless necessary."

Winter shook her head and went back to organizing the chairs. "Who in the world told you that?"

"Truth?" Autumn asked.

"Yes."

Autumn averted her eyes to the ceiling. "I may have followed him around for a little bit while you were practicing with the models and overheard him telling the bar manager who likes you to keep his distance. Then he told that one model who asked you out that you would never date a guy who wore pink. He also turned down several requests from women who asked him out, saying that he was already in a relationship with someone. Oh, and I heard him tell the guy who's doing the lighting for the fashion show—who apparently has issues with feet—that you caught some type of incurable foot fungus thing that you picked up in Hawaii."

Winter shot upright. "Say what! He said that? There's nothing wrong with my feet." Before she knew it, her heels were crossing the room so she could give

Taheim a piece of her mind about spreading unnecessary rumors.

"Yes, but that's not the point." Autumn caught her by the arm and turned her in the opposite direction. "The point is, Taheim likes you. I mean *really* likes you. And I can only assume that you're the one trying to keep your relationship under wraps. Clearly, he would probably tell every guy involved in the Inferno grand opening that you are his girlfriend and every woman who's interested in him to take a hike. What gives?"

Winter glanced away, trying to figure out how to explain how she felt to her sister when she was still trying to work out how she felt herself. Just when she was about to speak, commotion by the bar got their attention.

"Who's that woman talking to Taheim?" Autumn asked. "She's pretty."

"I don't know." She observed the woman with long brown hair, a tiny waist and smooth caramel skin talking with Taheim. "By his body language, I take it he doesn't want to talk to her."

"Ohh," Autumn said when the woman tried to touch Taheim's arm and he yanked it from her. "Whoever she is, she's really making him upset."

"She is…" Her words trailed off as she caught Taheim's gaze. The frustrated look in his eyes told her everything she needed to know.

"I know who she is."

"Who?"

She felt a huge knot in her stomach that grew larger the longer she watched the interaction. "That's Andrea, Taheim's ex-fiancée."

"Do you know what she wants?"

Winter sighed. *Guess the honeymoon's over.* "If I had to guess, I'd say she's here to tell Taheim that her eight-year-old son may be his and to try and win him back."

"Goodness," Autumn hissed before looking over at Winter. "You know what this means?"

"What?" Winter asked, unable to tear her eyes away from Taheim and Andrea.

"This means time's up. You've got to tell Taheim how you feel about him."

"Easier said than done."

Taheim squeezed his forehead to try to ease his growing headache. He was going off three hours of sleep and the last way he wanted to spend his night was cooped up in a coffee shop talking to Andrea. However, when she had popped up at Inferno, all he could think about was dragging her out of there before she caused a scene. The coffee shop down the street was the best option.

What in the world did I ever see in her? She was nothing like Winter. Everything about Andrea screamed fake. Sure, looks-wise, she was attractive, and to some men, it wouldn't even matter that the personality didn't match her looks. Even her makeup seemed caked on. As though if he scrubbed her face clean, he'd find Made in China stamped across her forehead.

"If you want to see your son, you have to come to Florida."

"Stop calling him my son. You have no idea if he's mine."

"News flash. If he wasn't my ex-husband's, then he's yours."

It wasn't that Taheim didn't think it was a possibility her son was his. In fact, he knew it was a very strong possibility. But all he could think about when she referred to her son as his was spending the next ten years of his life dealing with her.

"I don't want to meet him until after a DNA test to confirm he's my child."

"He's getting an award in school for his science project. I want you there for that."

"Andrea, I'm not entering his life without confirmation first. And I don't have to be in Florida to get a test."

She rolled her eyes in irritation. "What the hell happened to you?"

"Me? You're the one acting crazy."

"Just because I want my son to know his father, doesn't make me crazy."

"If you wanted him to know his father, you would have told me about him eight years ago and you wouldn't have kept him a secret from your ex-husband."

She crossed her hands over her chest. "Look at you, in Chicago acting like you're somebody. You must have forgot who made you the man you are today."

"I refuse to have this argument with you, Andrea."

"Don't act like you can't tolerate me." She gave him a smile that he assumed was supposed to be sexy. "Because from what I remember, you can handle me just fine."

"If you really felt that way, you wouldn't have cheated on me." He immediately shook his head, thinking he definitely didn't want to go there. It didn't matter anymore.

"I made a mistake," she said. "Haven't you ever made a mistake or regretted a situation that you couldn't take back?"

An image of his first date with Winter flashed in his head. "Of course I have. It's called being human. But there's a difference between making a one-time mistake and having an affair for years."

She dropped her head to the table before lifting it back up. "Will you ever forgive me?"

"You're forgiven."

"You said it too fast for me to believe you," she whined as she poked her lips out. "We were together for ten years. There has to be a part of you that still loves me."

For a couple years after their breakup, Taheim had tried to convince himself that he wasn't in love with Andrea. He wanted to prove to himself that he could move on. Then somewhere along the line, he'd realized that he was over her. He'd realized that he was better off without her.

The heart was a funny thing. Looking back on his years with Andrea, he wondered if he'd spent so many years with her because he was comfortable with her. Being with Andrea had been easy at the time, and not because she was an easy person to deal with. It was because dealing with her was something he'd done for so long he didn't know any different. He didn't see past the drama, the constant lying. It was those rare moments when she'd curl up in his arms and they'd sit in silence that kept him with her. Those moments when he felt as if she needed someone to lean on and talk to. Her own hero.

"You're right. It wasn't all bad."

She smiled. "Do you remember when we pulled that prank in Mr. Picklers's class?"

"How could I forget? He was so upset at us for convincing the entire class to participate in the Y2K the-world-is-coming-to-an-end fiasco."

"Watching him duck under his desk while we had those fireworks go off outside the window was priceless."

"I don't think he ever forgave us for that. I ran into him a few years ago and he could barely look me in the eye."

They shared a laugh. He meant what he said. It hadn't all been bad. However, until he met Winter, he hadn't known that he was still letting Andrea control his life. He was still letting her betrayal consume him. Winter was right. He'd allowed her to take too much of him.

"We had some good times, but there's no part of me that still loves you."

Her face went from happy to insulted in a matter of seconds. "That's what you think."

"That's what I know. We were friends at some point in our lives and I think it's best if we try to be cordial during this process. Until I figure out if your child is my son."

"How can you do that?" she said in frustration. "How can you think about the good times and still blow me off like you can't still feel something between us? This shit is really starting to piss me off."

"You've wasted enough of my time." He glanced at his watch. "You know what I really remember when I think of you? I remember ignoring the snide remarks you'd make about the clothes I used to design for my-self in college. You recall those comments, right? The ones about me never making it as a designer. Then I think about how many warnings I ignored in our re-lationship. Like that time I caught you leaving Mr. French's class during study hall adjusting your dress. Then I remember how you told me nothing was going on and I believed you. Not because I didn't think some-thing was going on. It was because he was a teacher and you were an underage student and I didn't want to be the type of guy to ruin a man's career and a girl's reputation. And you know what I remember the most of all?"

He watched the rage slowly build in her eyes and continued talking. "What I remember most of all was the way you looked at me when I found you in our home…our home that I'd worked my ass off to afford…with another man. And not just any man. A man I trusted. A man I knew. With the woman I thought I would spend the rest of my life with. I was a popular guy and there were so many times I could have cheated on you with someone else. But I didn't, because commitment, even at a young age, was im-portant to me."

She rolled her eyes as she called the waiter over to refill her coffee. "You always were way too sen-sitive for me." Her words should have cut. They should have made him feel something. Anything. Even anger. But he didn't feel a thing. She was so selfish. Self-centered. Mean-spirited.

"I don't expect you to understand. Hell, I really don't give a shit what you take from this conversa-tion. But I was never a sensitive man, and trust me, being around you made my skin thicker than ten layers of concrete. What's really sad is that in that warped mind of yours, you don't realize that the emotion you believed made me weak, the quality that you couldn't figure out…was me loving you. Because unlike you, I've always wanted that. I've always wanted a woman who'd uplift me when I needed it. Soothe me when I hurt. Make love to me in that moment when we both had such a bad day that the only thing we could think of was coming home and ripping each other's clothes off. I believe in romance. And you…" He leaned closer to be clear she heard him. "Well, you'll spend the rest of your life still trying to figure out exactly what our conversation was about tonight."

A chime at the door got her attention. Taheim didn't have to turn to see what she had her eyes on. It was obviously a man. She was batting her eyes hard enough to give everyone in the coffee shop whiplash.

"If you're done rattling on about whatever you just were, I think it's best that I tell you that the online gossip mag, you know, the one that was so eager to print our love story years ago? Well, they are eager to hear what else I want to discuss with them about you." She pulled a photo out of her purse and slid it across the table at him. "Meaning your son. This was taken a couple months ago."

As Taheim studied the photo, his heart began beating out of his chest. It wasn't as if he were meeting the boy in person yet. It was only a photo. But it was a strange feeling that consumed him as he stared into the eyes of a child who could be his. A young boy with a short fade and a huge smile who'd spent the past eight years of his life without a father, without a man to look up to as a role model.

"Oh, and before you tell me again that you aren't coming to Florida, I guess I should let you read this." She handed him a piece of paper she'd pulled out when she'd gotten the photo. As Taheim began reading the first paragraphs, he immediately balled the paper up.

"What the fuck is this?"

"I figured that would get your attention." She flicked her hair over her shoulder and winked at someone at the counter. Probably the same guy she'd winked at before. "It's the draft of what I will send to the magazine if you don't accompany me to Florida this week. In case you didn't get to the good stuff, it states that when you found out I was pregnant, you checked me into a mental facility."

"I talked to your ex. He said your mother told him that you had been suicidal during your pregnancy, which is why you were in that clinic."

"Oh, please." She waved off his words. "It's crazy what a homeless guy will do for a little change. I paid him to sign your name on my documents to enroll me, and my mom sat back and watched me do it. Your name is on everything."

"Forgery is illegal and there's no doubt that your case would never hold up in court."

"I have enough dirt on my mom and ex to convince them to stay quiet. Call it a benefit of surrounding yourself with people just as fucked up as you. Whatever my ex told you, he'd never testify and neither would my mother. Besides, the magazine doesn't give a shit about that. A story is a story, and by the time you figure out how to take legal action against me, I'll already have accomplished my goal."

The smile plastered across her face made his stomach turn. Visions of how many people would find out about Andrea's latest stunt if he involved the courts were enough to make him contemplate her request. He was tired of involving his family and friends in his drama with her. He was smarter now. Wiser. He'd done a lot of growing after they broke up and he'd be damned if he let her undo any of that. *Or jeopardize my possible future with Winter.*

"This conversation is over." He threw a few bills on the table and stood to leave.

"Should I email this to them now?" she called behind him.

He turned and looked her up and down in disgust. "I'll see you in Florida."

Chapter 18

"Thanks and have a nice day." Winter wasn't sure how many customers had walked through the store today, but she was really tired of plastering on a smile.

"Has he called you yet?" Autumn asked.

"Not yet."

"I'm sure he'll call," Danni added.

Winter gave them a look of disbelief. "Three days ago he tells me that he's going to Florida with his ex to get a DNA test and I haven't heard from him since. The odds are not in my favor."

"Did you tell him how you feel?" Autumn asked.

"Where did I have the time to fit that in? Oh, I know." She snapped her fingers. "Right in between *Winter, I have to go to Florida* and *I'll finally confirm if he's my son.* You're so right. Following that up with *Okay, I really care about you, so call me when you get there—tell me everything* would have worked perfectly."

"Well, not like that," Danni said, shaking her head. "Besides, isn't what you feel for him a little stronger than you're letting on?"

Winter averted her eyes from the two women trying to read into her behavior. "No, I just care about him."

"Oh, honey, we aren't stupid. It's obvious how much you care about him. Otherwise, you wouldn't care that he hasn't called."

"I only care because the fashion show is in two days." She started busying herself by straightening up random objects on the checkout counter. "She was pretty. Autumn, you noticed how she looked at him when she walked into Inferno."

"From how Taheim looked, she's not pretty where it counts. All I noticed that night was the fact that he wasn't looking at her like she was looking at him. He was too busy looking at you."

Deep down, Winter had thought the same thing. "He was in love with her once. He'd pledged to spend the rest of his life with her."

"Didn't she betray him, though?" Danni asked. "And now there's a possibility that she kept his son from him? Seems like he dodged a bullet, if you ask me."

Winter agreed—of course he'd dodged a bullet. But who was to say he wouldn't dodge a bullet with her? Some people were easy to love, while others… Well, others just weren't.

Autumn walked over and placed her hand on her shoulder. "Please tell me that you aren't holding back with telling Taheim how you feel because of Mom and how she treated you growing up."

Winter blinked back tears when Autumn nailed the exact reason that had been haunting her mind since she'd realized she was falling for Taheim.

"Winter, you can't let her impact your future of happiness." Autumn pulled her in for a hug. "You spent years trying to please that woman, but sometimes we just have to let people be who they are, and in this case, Mom will always be Mom. Selfish. Greedy. And hell-bent on trying to break you any way she can."

Winter wiped away a couple tears, irritated at herself for even shedding them. "What if..." she said as her voice slightly cracked. "What if I got more from Mom than just my physical features? What if she was right and I'm destined to turn into her? She wasn't always who she is today. When Dad met her, she was a different person...a lot like the person I am now."

"Listen to me, sis," Autumn said, grabbing her with both hands. "Even if you tried, you will never be that woman. The only thing she ever did for us was bring us into this world. You will *never* turn into the type of woman she is. The sooner you realize that, the sooner you can open your heart up to love and give Taheim the chance that you've failed to give every man who ever wanted to win your heart. I think that all the crap Mom put you through was preparing you for this moment. Time to finally stop being there for others and let someone take care of you. *Love* you. Cherish you."

Winter soaked in her sister's words, feeling the truth in them. She'd never let fear hold her back in any other aspect of her life, so she definitely didn't need to start now.

"Thanks, Autumn. I know you're right," she said, wiping away a few more tears. "Even if he doesn't feel the same way about me, I have to tell him how I feel."

Autumn glanced over at Danni before the two shared a laugh.

"What is it?" Winter asked as she looked from one to the other.

"Sweetie, you're so dense when it comes to Taheim," Autumn said, shaking her head. "How many times have I told you this since you returned from your trip? If it were up to Taheim, he would already have I'm in Love with Winter Dupree tattooed across his chest."

Winter smiled, hoping they were right.

Taheim stared at the thin piece of paper in his hand. It barely had any weight to it, proof that the weight of the paper wasn't important to the DNA center. The most important factor about the sheet of paper was the information printed on it. The black font seemed to rise off the pages and slap him across the face.

"You can stare at it all you want," Ajay said as he walked over to his brother and placed a comforting hand on his shoulder. "The words on the sheet will still be the same."

"I know," he replied as he folded the sheet and placed it in a secure place. "I just can't believe it. That's all."

His trip to Florida had lasted a little longer than he'd thought. He had intended to be there only two rather than four days but had ended up getting back today, a day before the fashion show.

"You shouldn't be here," he said to Ajay. "You have a grand opening to prepare for."

Ajay shrugged. "Most of it is planned. Besides, you're the one who's been gone a few days. Don't you need to prepare for the show?"

"Yeah, but I plan on pulling an all-nighter."

"Even so, you need to rest. A lot has happened recently." His brother squinted his eyes in observation. "Paternity test aside, how do you feel about Andrea? Did seeing her dig up any old feelings?"

Taheim sat on the edge of his desk as he thought about their meeting in the coffee shop and the craziness he'd had to deal with in Florida.

Just as he'd predicted, Andrea had wasted no time trying to get him in her bed. She'd even gone so far as to beg her mom to bring her son to the hotel they were staying at—in separate rooms—and then she'd waited in the lobby for him with the boy. He'd thought they were meeting in the restaurant of the hotel because his lawyers had finally gotten to her. After their meeting at the coffeehouse, he'd informed his legal team for Collegiate Life and T.R. Night about Andrea's accusations and her threat to bring the information to a gossip magazine. They'd immediately jumped to action.

When he arrived at the restaurant and noticed the boy with Andrea, he'd wanted to immediately turn around, but she was already calling out to him. He'd still walked away, but she'd caught him at the elevator.

She'd introduced him to Jamar, and his face had

cringed when she mentioned that he was her son. He wasn't sure how often Andrea had seen Jamar, since she lived in Texas, but he assumed it wasn't a lot based on the strained look on Jamar's face.

"I didn't feel a thing," Taheim said, finally answering his brother's question. "Not even a hint of attraction or love or any friendly feelings whatsoever. If anything, I felt sorry for her."

Ajay smirked in relief. "I'm glad to hear that, bro." He gave him a suggestive look. "So does that mean you've decided to be open about your feelings for a certain brown beauty who's caused you to lose focus on more than one occasion?"

Taheim smiled at his brother's not-so-subtle question. "If you're asking me if I've decided to tell Winter how I feel about her, then the answer is yes, I'm definitely going to tell her how I feel."

"And how exactly do you feel?"

His lips curled into a side smile as he thought about how exciting his life had been since he'd met her. Whether they were disagreeing about something, participating in a questionable theatrical show, diving off a rocky cliff or stealing kisses when they thought no one was looking, he knew that a life without Winter wouldn't be a life worth living.

"I love her, man. More than I thought I could ever love somebody. And it's not that passing kind of love. It's the kind that I secretly always wanted but never thought I'd find. The unconditional kind of love. More important, she accepts me for me and she's beautiful inside and out. She didn't turn her back at Andrea's accusations, but instead she offered me support, no matter my decision."

Ajay's mouth turned into a wide smile. "So when exactly are you going to profess this unconditional love you speak of?"

Taheim grinned. "I was hoping you'd ask that question."

Chapter 19

Winter peeked her head out the red velvet curtain to gaze at the sea of people wearing an array of different masquerade masks. She smiled at the number of people who continued to admire the place in awe despite the fact that they'd probably been there for hours. Elite Events had really outdone themselves with the decor. Inferno felt more like a holiday fantasy than a lounge.

Every waiter and waitress wore all black and had on the same mask with the word Inferno interlaced in the design. She'd heard that Elite Events had found a vendor to make the masks unique to the Inferno Lounge.

They had also set up numerous photo backdrop sections throughout the massive two-level venue, as well as hired photographers, who clicked away, giving patrons more than enough opportunity to capture the perfect shot of the night.

Long shimmery pieces of silver fabric entwined with lines of crystals were delicately placed throughout the lounge. The ceiling was draped in the same luscious red velvet as the curtain that separated the models backstage from the crowd.

She had to admit, Ajay had really outdone himself with the opening. She hadn't attended the grand openings of many of his lounge and club locations, mainly because they had already been open when she moved to Chicago. But she couldn't imagine they'd gone as well as this event was going. He was setting trends and taking names, daring any Chicago club owner to top the event he had.

She glanced back at the models and smiled at the pieces she and Taheim had created for the night. Fabrics in holiday colors filled the backstage area. The masks that all the models wore just added to the mystery and enticement of their attire. She was completely satisfied with each piece of lingerie that was walking out onstage tonight and she'd be the first to admit Taheim's all-nighters had really paid off. There was no doubt in her mind that his T.R. Night collection would be another successful clothing line.

At the sound of the DJ signaling for attendees to take their seats for the fashion show, she glanced around for Taheim and was not surprised to find him already looking at her. But there was something else in his eyes, something she couldn't make out. He almost looked sneaky standing on the other side of the room wearing a sly smile on his face.

I wonder what he's up to. Unfortunately, she wouldn't be able to ask until after the show.

* * *

With each piece that walked across the stage, Taheim's chest swelled with pride. The crowd was really enjoying the fashion show and he loved the way his and Winter's interpretations of lingerie and nightwear favored one another.

Both the collections had something for everyone. Winter's holiday collection included seductive teddies, sweet satin camis, jaw-dropping boy shorts and bikini panties. Pieces such as Sugary Kisses, Tender Mistletoe and Sensual Silver Bell got a range of *ohhs* and *aahs*. Every piece was better than the last. Her black-velvet-with-red-trimmings set, which she called Naughty Little Santa, was a huge crowd-pleaser.

While her collection was seducing the audience, Taheim's collection brought a little more edge. His silk collection of robes, pants, shirts and shorts were standard men's nightwear. Although they were typical in type, each style had that T.R. Night edge. He was the most excited about the crowd's reaction to his Deep in the Night pieces...the collection that he had been inspired to create after coming back from Vegas and Hawaii.

Deep in the Night was for the bolder man, the man who didn't want to sleep in just anything. He wanted to make a statement even in his sleep, even in the darkest hour of the night. The collection included knit pants, shorts, boxers and briefs with words on the waistband like Powerful, Arrogant, Calculated, Ladies' Man, Innovative Thinker, and Society's Nightmare. The purpose behind the collection was to represent the personality of a man and his freedom to express himself even underneath his clothing. For laughs, he'd thrown in some briefs with a few holiday sayings like Jingle My Bells, Let's Be Naughty and, his personal favorite, No Peeking 'til Christmas.

When the fashion show was over, he glanced over at Winter, whose happiness was reflected in her eyes, in her smile and in the way she did a little jump for joy.

The models all did their final walk and the announcer called for the designers to take the stage. *Here goes nothing*, he thought as he surprised Winter by taking her hand before they walked out onstage. He knew that she expected them to take a bow at the end, wave to the audience and head backstage. Little did she know there'd been a change of plans. He nodded for the announcer to leave the stage and pulled two microphones out of his blazer. He clicked them on and handed one to her.

It was almost impossible to keep his composure when he noticed the look of confusion—and a little bit of panic—on her face. "Ajay wants us to say something instead." Not one to be unprofessional, she quickly nodded her head and smiled to the audience.

"Ladies and gentlemen, we just wanted to personally thank you for giving us a chance to share our lingerie and nightwear collections with you this evening at the grand masquerade gala for Inferno Lounge." He clapped his hands and the crowd roared and clapped along with him.

"As designers, we create for you," Winter said, waving her hand to the audience. "We create because it's our passion, our destiny, our duty to bring you magnificent, one-of-a-kind pieces unique to today's trends."

I should have known she would just jump right in.

"See, that's what I admire most about Winter Dupree, ladies and gentlemen. A minute ago I told her we had to speak to the audience before we left the stage and she didn't hesitate to grab the mic and speak from her heart."

She smiled, but her eyes were pleading for him to tell her what was going on.

"You see, I brought Winter onstage because I lost a dare." She squinted her eyes together in confusion. He winked at her before turning toward the audience again.

"We had a social media battle and I told her that I had won and she had lost, when in actuality, I was the one who lost."

"You're kidding me," she said into the mic. "You cheated?"

"Not how you think. You were right. The only reason I won is that I implied that there was something more going on between us and my tweet blew up."

"Ah, I see. Well, I still believe that is exactly why you won."

"It is, so I figured a public apology was in order."

She shook her head with a laugh when he grabbed her free hand. "Winter Dupree, I am so sorry for tweeting that message to solidify my win for our bet. And I apologize for thinking that you are the sexiest woman I've ever met with the biggest heart I've ever seen."

Her eyes got bigger and the crowd, which had been cheering him on, grew quiet.

"I'm sorry that you're the main star of all my naughty fantasies…" That got a few howls out of the audience. "And I'm sorry that even when I'm supposed to be working, I can't help but think about you."

"You ain't lying," his friend Jaleen yelled from his seat. Winter's gaze didn't falter.

"I'm sorry that I'm a better man when I'm around you and I'm extra sorry that we understand each other and connect in ways I'd never imagined."

Taheim hadn't really contemplated how his entire speech would play out, but now that he was onstage putting his feelings on display for his friends, family and damn near all of Chicago to see, there was no stopping what he would say next.

"And most of all, I'm sorry that I fell in love with you, because I'm sure you never saw that coming." She searched his eyes before her mouth curled in a smile.

"But you should be sorry, too." He raised an eyebrow at her, which got a few laughs from the audience. His face grew more serious as the laughter subsided. Her hand tightened in his and he wondered if she suspected his next move. Only his Winter would know what he was going to do next. *His*... He liked the sound of that.

"You should be sorry that you taught me how to be more spontaneous, because had you let that side of me remain hidden, I'm sure you would have gotten a much better proposal."

She gasped and her eyes filled with tears. "Are you proposing?" If her mouth hadn't been close to the microphone, he wasn't sure he would have heard her.

"You bet your ass I'm proposing," he said with a smile. "Guess our secret's out in the open."

She glanced around the audience before swiping a few tears from her eyes. "I guess you're right." She turned back to him wearing the sexiest smile he'd ever seen.

"I love you more than my next breath, Taheim Reed. You may make me laugh and make me cry, and you're right—I will never understand how this happened." She pointed her hand from him to her and the crowd erupted in laughter.

"But I know that there isn't anyone I'd rather fight with or laugh with…or even cry with than you." The eyes locked to his were full of emotion.

Feeling like the moment had arrived, Taheim kneeled on one knee.

"So my question to you, Winter Dupree, is… Will you marry me so we can continue to fight and love one another? Assuming that the fighting results in makeup sex?"

She playfully hit him on the arm as the crowd laughed. "I'd love the honor of being your wife, so my answer is an absolute yes."

Taheim's lips were on hers in seconds. The crowd was going crazy, and right on cue, the DJ began playing music and the staff began clearing the chairs off the floor to offer more space. As he stood onstage kissing Winter, his fiancée, he realized that after years of searching for happiness, he had finally found it… in Winter.

Four hours passed before they were able to sneak away from Inferno and head to Taheim's condo. Now, in Taheim's SUV on the short ten-minute drive, she felt it was still ten minutes too long.

"Are we crazy for getting engaged?"

"Yes," she said with a laugh.

"Are you happy?" His voice was hesitant, as if he wasn't sure what she'd say.

"I couldn't be happier." She leaned over to him and placed her lips on his cheek.

"Sorry I proposed without a ring. We can pick one up tomorrow unless you want me to surprise you with the one I saw last week that reminded me of you."

Her heart swelled at the fact that he'd actively looked at rings. "You can surprise me, but there is no need to apologize. The ring is just an object. Having your love is enough."

"Damn, I love you," he said with a laugh before his face grew serious. "There's something I have to tell you. Something I should have told you right when I landed back in Chicago yesterday."

"What is it?"

He glanced at her before returning his eyes to the road. "The DNA test results came back for Andrea's son."

Ah, now I understand his change of mood. "Taheim, I knew it was a possibility and I'm fine with that. The only thing I don't like about the situation is the fact that you've been away from him for eight years."

The relief on Taheim's face was immediate. "That's another reason why I love you. You'd love me even if you had to deal with a crazy baby mama like Andrea?"

"Of course," she said with a smile. He returned her smile.

"Well, no worries, because he's not my son."

"What!" Winter shrieked. "So she was sleeping around on you and her ex?"

"Sure was," Taheim said with a laugh.

"Um, why do you think this is funny? The nerve of her."

Taheim placed his hand on Winter's knee. "I'm laughing because I don't care about her enough to be pissed, and to be honest, I dodged a bullet because she would have been hard for both of us to deal with."

"I could have handled her," Winter said defensively. "In fact, I wish I could give her a piece of my mind."

"How about we forget about her and never talk about her again?"

"Works for me," she said with a smile. She waited until he was focused on the road again before she studied his features. "Then what's upsetting you?"

He stole a glance in her direction. "It's going to sound crazy."

"Try me."

He didn't speak right away. "I was looking forward to being a father. I definitely didn't want to have to deal with Andrea's crazy ass, but I realized how much I wanted children of my own."

She nodded her head in understanding as she placed her hand over his hand, which was resting on her leg. "If you hadn't been disappointed, you wouldn't be the man I know you are. There's nothing wrong with the way you're feeling. And I definitely want a lot of children, so you just happen to be in luck."

He gave her a sly smile as he pulled into the parking garage of his building. "I know we just got engaged, but you want to start practicing on making those babies?"

She playfully swatted him on the arm. "Is your mind always in the gutter?"

"Baby, I'm sorry, but there will never be a time

that I'm not thinking about spreading you out on the bed and making love to you…cherishing your mind and body. I mean, you create sexy lingerie for a living and you expect me to think about anything else?"

She suddenly remembered a very important part about the night that had slipped her mind. "Which reminds me. We have to get out of this car and head to your bedroom so I can show you what I have for you."

His eyes lifted enticingly. "Is it something under your dress? Something I can take off…preferably with my teeth." He nuzzled his face in the crook of her neck.

"Maybe," she said breathlessly as he began trailing kisses along her collarbone.

"Is it something with lace?" His hand slipped in between her thighs.

"Yes." Her voice sounded far away, as if she were yelling down a long hallway.

"Hmm, I like where this is going." Without further warning, his hand cupped her and he rubbed his thumb up and down her center. Her moans filled the car, mingling with his grunts. "Tell me what it is, and I'll stop torturing you so we can finish this in my condo."

Her mouth curved to form a sentence, but words escaped her when his fingers stopped rubbing on the outside of the material and slipped past the band of her thong.

"Taheim," she breathed. "It's the lingerie from that night."

His fingers slowed slightly. "What night?"

"The night in your condo. The night you walked into your bedroom and saw me standing there. I'm wearing it."

His eyes flew to hers and what she saw in them literally stole her breath. There was no laughter. No playfulness. No amusement. His gaze was lethal, unapologetic and consuming every part of her. She'd unleashed the beast he was trying to hold back and her body quivered in excitement at what was yet to come.

With skill and precision that made her gasp in surprise, he eased them both into the backseat to give them more space.

"There's no way I can wait," he said as he expertly began removing their clothes. Winter didn't know how to process how much pleasure she was feeling, but she also realized that she didn't need to process anything. All she needed to do was *feel*. And so she did. She let go of everything except for the way that Taheim was making her feel.

"This is the beginning of the rest of our lives," he whispered in her ear. She didn't respond. She didn't need to. Her body did all the talking. Best. Night. *Ever*.

* * * * *

REQUEST YOUR FREE BOOKS!

2 FREE NOVELS
PLUS 2 FREE GIFTS!

KIMANI™
ROMANCE

Love's ultimate destination!

KROM15

The first two stories in the *Love in the Limelight* series, where four unstoppable women find fame, fortune and ultimately… true love.

LOVE IN THE LIMELIGHT

New York Times bestselling author

BRENDA JACKSON

&

A.C. ARTHUR

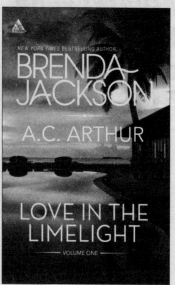

In *Star of His Heart,* Ethan Chambers is Hollywood's most eligible bachelor. But when he meets his costar Rachel Wellesley, he suddenly finds himself thinking twice about staying single.

In *Sing Your Pleasure,* Charlene Quinn has just landed a major contract with L.A.'s hottest record label, working with none other than Akil Hutton. Despite his gruff attitude, she finds herself powerfully attracted to the driven music producer.

Available now wherever books are sold!

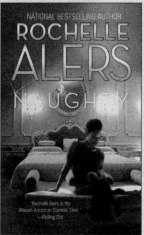